GRIZZLE'S ~~ST GRIZELDA'S~~ SCHOOL FOR GIRLS, GEEKS AND TAG-ALONG ZOMBIES

KAREN McCOMBIE

Illustrated by BECKA MOOR

stripes

For William Baldwin and Karine
                              — KMcC

        To the Lofthousers
                        — BM

PROPERTY OF:

ST GRIZZLE'S
SCHOOL FOR GIRLS

Kindly on loan to

NAME	YEAR
Clementine Bunce	1921
Sybil Lemon	1947
Primrose Poppleton	1960
Hermione O'Hanrahanan	2001

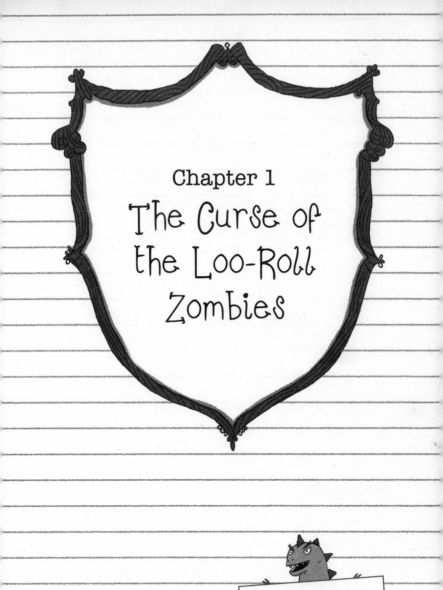

Chapter 1
The Curse of the Loo-Roll Zombies

And the mystery of my BFF's silence...

WHACK!

POP!

Ffffttt...

The **WHACK!** is the sound of the dorm door being shoved open and smacking against the wall.

The **POP!** is my one and only dorm-mate Swan blowing and snapping a pink bubble of gum as she pads into the room, her fresh-from-the-shower hair leaving a trail of drips on the floor behind her.

The **Ffffttt...** might sound like a deflating air bed but it's actually Swan letting out a long, weary sigh, which comes with a matching eyeroll.

"What?" I say, blinking over at her from the bottom bunk I'm sitting on.

It's Wednesday morning, it's five minutes to breakfast and I was halfway through getting ready when I got distracted. Swan is probably sighing and rolling her eyes at the sight of me still in my PJs with one side of my hair neatly plaited and the other a mess of sticky-out brown frizz. Oh, and I've just remembered I've got my toothbrush tucked behind my left ear.

"You're not watching that film AGAIN, are you, Dani?" Swan asks, nodding at the mobile phone I'm holding in my lap.

Right, so it's got nothing to do with my effortless lack of style. She's talking about the mini-movie my best friend Arch posted on our YouTube channel on Sunday night.

"Well, yeah," I answer with a shrug.

"How many times have you viewed it now?" asks Swan as she starts slamming around in drawers, looking for some clothes.

"Not that many," I lie.

Thirty-three times, actually, I realize, glancing down at the counter on the YouTube page.

Since I arrived at St Grizzle's, me and my back-at-home buddy Arch are usually in touch every day, sometimes several times a day, by messaging and texts and video chats. But most of all, we make and upload dumb-but-fun mini-movies for each other to watch.

I last uploaded one on Saturday – it was a James Bond action scene, from the movie *Sceptre*. I made a tiny tuxedo out of black tissue paper for my little plastic brontosaurus, then dangled the dinosaur from Swan's twin brother Zed's remote-controlled helicopter with a bit of gift-wrap ribbon I found in the art room. While I filmed, Zed expertly flew the helicopter, making Secret Agent Dino 007 swoop and zip around the back lawn of the school.

It was excellent, even AFTER the helicopter crash-landed in a rhododendron bush and Swan had to rescue it and Secret Agent Dino 007 before Twinkle the school goat leaped in and ate them. (Actually, that was the BEST bit.)

My James Bond tribute was in reply to a mini-movie Arch had posted a couple of days earlier of himself having a conversation with a sock puppet. I only sussed that the sock was meant to be ME when I spotted the brown wool plaits he'd attached to either side with safety pins.

It was so funny, especially when another sock puppet – made to look like my dog Downboy – **boing**ed into the frame and chased sock-puppet Dani round the table.

11

And it got even funnier when my old teacher, Miss Solomon, loomed into shot behind Arch saying, "Well, THIS doesn't look much like converting fractions to decimals to ME, Archie Kaminski!" before yanking BOTH the socks off his hands in one swift move. (Guess filming in class was a pretty stupid idea...)

So, yeah, fun mini-movies are our thing.

Only this latest mini-movie of Arch's is not funny, not a bit.

"Are you still convinced there's something up with him?" asks Swan, pulling a T-shirt down over her wet head.

"Kind of," I say, nibbling at the skin around my nail while I stare at the screen – and wonder if I'll have time to play it for the thirty-fourth time before we have to go down to the dining room.

Here's the thing – Arch's latest mini-movie stars zombies made out of loo-roll tubes.

He's drawn goggle-eyed zombie faces on the cardboard tubes and given them outstretched arms using wooden lolly sticks. But these living-dead creatures are not exactly cute and they don't really do much.

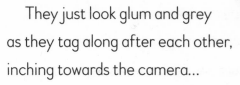

They just look glum and grey as they tag along after each other, inching towards the camera...

"Still not made contact?" asks Swan as she fastens the shoulder straps on her cut-off dungarees.

"Nope. It's been days now," I reply. "It's so unlike him. I've left comments on this film, I've texted him, I've tried to video chat, I've called his mobile..."

I pause, thinking how strange it was to hear

Arch's usual, cheerful, "Sorry, I can't take your call right now cos I've been abducted by aliens!" message. Because of the gloomy zombies and the silence, I'm starting to think he might be feeling not-very-cheerful-at-**all** in REAL life.

"...so I've basically tried every way I can to get in touch with him," I continue, since Swan's staring at me in that unsettlingly stern way of hers. "Every way except..."

This time I've stopped cos I'm thinking about what I might have to do as a last resort.

"Except what?" asks Swan, staring harder.

"Except for calling him on his *home* phone," I tell her, my voice all rumbly-grumbly with dread.

The trouble is, one of Arch's parents is BOUND to pick up, and they have been SO weird towards me since I left, a whole not-quite-a-month ago.

Mr Kaminski – Arch's normally joke-a-minute

dad – sounds all sad and forlorn whenever he answers the phone to me now, like I am a condemned prisoner who's been given a life sentence, instead of an eleven-year-old girl who's having to spend a term at St Grizelda's School for Girls while her mum's on an exciting expedition to the Antarctic.

Mrs Kaminski is even WORSE. I swear she sounds all choked and teary whenever she talks to me. She totally doesn't approve of Mum sending her beloved only child away to boarding school. (To be honest, when I first heard Mum's plan to send me here, *I* didn't approve of it either – but that was before I fell for its random kooky charms.)

And even though I've tried to explain what it's ACTUALLY like here, Mrs Kaminski doesn't seem to believe that St Grizzle's really isn't a strict 'n' stern, no-fun, no-magic version of Hogwarts.

I mean, if only she could see the stone statue of St Grizelda out in the driveway at the front of the school... This morning she has an orange Christmas-cracker paper hat taped to her head and a slightly frayed, lime-green skipping rope dangling from her hands.

If only Mrs Kaminski could meet Lulu the head teacher, in her uniform of cut-off denim shorts, an old faded T-shirt and flip-flops with giant plastic daisies on them.

If only she could see the goblin flying past the dorm window on a trapeze right now, screaming its head off (in other words, eight-year-old Blossom from Newts Class getting ready for our upcoming lesson in circus skills).

But of course Mr and Mrs Kaminski's opinions of my new school don't matter as much as

discovering what's going on
with my friend Arch.

Is he really, truly as
gloomy as his loo-roll zombies?

Like James (Brontosaurus) Bond,
it's my mission to find out...

Chapter 2
Boo!

And
AAAARRRRGGHHH!

"Oi, Dani – are you trying to start a new trend?" mutters Swan.

I glance up from the list I'm making to see what Swan's on about.

She's sitting next to me, slouching across the desk and pointing at my forehead.

"What is it?" whispers Zed, leaning over from his wheelchair on the other side of me.

"She's got a blob of toothpaste on her eyebrow," says Swan, keeping her voice JUST low enough so Miss Amethyst doesn't hear.

I quickly rub away the dried white gloop with the sleeve of my cardie. This morning – after spending WAY too long staring at loo-roll zombies – I'd got dressed and ready for breakfast at lightning speed. Only I was hurrying so much that when I yanked on my T-shirt I forgot to take the toothbrush out from behind my ear and got in a bit of a tangle.

"So that's been there all through breakfast and assembly?" I hiss. "Why didn't you tell me?"

"Cos it was funny?" Swan suggests with a shrug.

"AAAARRRRGGHHH!"

Me, Swan, Zed – and even Miss Amethyst – pay absolutely NO attention to the blood-curdling yelp coming from another part of the school.

We're not being uncaring, it's just that we know for sure that nothing is actually *wrong* with the yelper. It's Blossom, and she's just in a really grumpy mood and has been **"AAAARRRRGGHHH!"**ing at regular intervals ever since assembly, all because Lulu announced that today's schedule would have to be tweaked as she had a Very Important Meeting at 10 a.m.

So rather than having a whole-school circus skills session this morning, we were all splitting off to do other stuff. My Year 6 class (Fungi) would have an extra science lesson with Miss Amethyst, the Year 5 Conkers Class and Year 4 Otters were being taken into the woods by art teacher Mademoiselle Fabienne to draw woodlice, while Granny Viv – the newest employee at St Grizzle's and my ACTUAL granny – was going to give the Year 3 Newts a cookery lesson.

That's when Blossom let rip with her first, ear-splitting "**AAAARRRRGGHHH!**"

At first I'd thought Blossom might've had her toe run over by Zed's wheelchair (it happens sometimes) or that she'd been headbutted by Twinkle (it happens a **lot**) or she'd heard wrong and thought that they were cooking with woodlice or something (on second thoughts, Blossom would probably think that was pretty cool).

But when I looked round I saw...

a) Zed parked – quite innocently – right beside me

b) Twinkle at the back of the school hall chewing on something that looked suspiciously like one of the shiny new school brochures Lulu had just ordered, and

c) Blossom wearing her brand-new 'Super-Grrrl' PJs and sprinkles of glitter on her face, all ready for circus skills class.

22

So Blossom was obviously just "AAAARRRRGGHHH!"ing cos she was gutted that her excellent outfit and sparkles were going to go to waste...

"Now, stop your nonsense and just behave yourself!" the three of us hear Miss Amethyst suddenly snap and all sit bolt upright.

Luckily we see that our teacher's not talking to me, Swan or Zed – she's frowning at the class computer, which is refusing to play the film she wants to show us. I think she said it was about plant cells or sound waves or the earth's crustiness or something.

I wasn't really listening, to be honest – I was too busy thinking about zombie loo rolls and worrying about Arch. Apart from finding out about my toothpasted eyebrow, I've spent the last few minutes scribbling a To Do list for my mission but it's a bit rubbish...

MISSION PLAN

- ~~Text Arch loads~~ *done that already*
- ~~Leave messages~~ *done that too*
- ~~Email him~~ *done that heaps of times*
- ~~Stick comments on YouTube~~ *done that as well*
- ~~Call his home number~~ *urgh, don't want to...*

While Miss Amethyst is busy with misbehaving software, I scrunch up my useless plan.

"So what ARE you going to do about getting in touch with Arch, Dani?" asks Zed.

"She's going to phone his house, THAT'S what she's going to do," Swan says, reaching out to grab my mobile, which is sitting on the desk.

"No! Don't you dare!" I whisper, grabbing the phone back.

"Hey, I know! Why don't you make a really great mini-movie that Arch can't RESIST commenting on?" Zed suggests.

"Maybe..." I mumble as I start scrolling through photos of my best friend, missing him madly.

The trouble is, my brain is slightly frazzled with worry. If I can't even come up with a solid bullet-pointed plan for my mission, how am I going to get inspiration for a new film?

"Hey, who's that?" Zed whispers now, leaning closer. Swan leans in to look, too.

"It's Arch, of course," I whisper back. I've paused at a picture of my best buddy at the lido back home, where we went swimming in the summer holidays last year.

"No way! He looks totally different!" says Swan, almost forgetting to whisper, she's so surprised.

Swan and Zed have seen Arch ALMOST for real plenty of times now, either on the films he sends me or sometimes during our video chats.

But they have never seen him like this.

"Hey, Arch isn't wearing his baseball cap!" says Zed, suddenly realizing what's changed. "He looks so different. He **always** wears his baseball cap, doesn't he?"

I gaze at the image, at Arch's stunned expression and his short fair hair with the flop of long fringe covering his forehead. "He even tried to wear it in the pool," I say, memories flooding back. "But it came off every time he jumped in..."

"Arch looks totally WRONG without his hat. It's like seeing Yas without her uniform or Miss

Amethyst wearing a colour that's not purple," says Swan.

Yas in Conkers Class is the only pupil who still wears the old-style uniform that all the girls were expected to wear back when St Grizelda's was a properly posh and serious school. Even when Lulu gently tells her she doesn't have to and waves super-comfy jogging bottoms at her.

And Miss Amethyst? Well, I risk a quick glance up and see her wearing her typical wafty layers of mauve, lilac and violet. Only her face breaks the colour code – it's bright pink with annoyance.

Oh, and speaking of faces, there's Toshio's peering at us through the glass panel in the classroom door, his ever-present headphones circling his neck. Toshio is a Japanese student who Lulu is supposed to be teaching English to in exchange for him being the temporary school receptionist... Except she never seems to have the time, which leaves Toshio free to amuse himself by listening to shouty music and playing computer games in the school office. Still, blissfully happy as he is, Toshio's lack of language skills makes things very confusing for anyone expecting a useful response when they contact the school.

Last week a man in a van had turned up to deliver the new school brochures. Only Toshio had never heard the word "brochure" before and every time he tried to repeat it – "brushirrrrr!" – it got funnier and funnier. In the end he was giggling too much to sign the delivery form and one of the nine-year-old triplets from Otters Class had to do it for him.

"Hello," says Toshio now, opening the door and bowing apologetically to Miss Amethyst. "Lulu says Fungi must come, please."

"Oh, well, fine – off you go, dears," says
Miss Amethyst, running a hand wearily through
her lavender-coloured hair and glowering at the
computer as if she'd quite like to tap it with a
brick.

And so the three of us who make up Fungi
Class set off after Toshio down the corridor. On
the cool stone tiles, Swan's flip-flops flap, Zed's
wheels squeak like a rapping mouse and my bare
feet don't make a sound.

29

"So, what does our mum need us for?" Zed asks Toshio.

When Zed says "our mum", he is not including ME, of course, since MY mother is currently studying penguins' bottoms in Antartica (for SCIENCE not **fun** reasons). Lulu is not only the head teacher, she's also Swan and Zed's mum, which is why Zed is St Grizzle's School for Girls one random boy – a fact he is very proud of.

But in answer to Zed's question, Toshio turns to us and just says a single word:

"BOO!"

Huh...?

"**BOO!**" he repeats a bit louder.

Me, Swan and Zed swap puzzled frowns.

But there's no time to ask Toshio the original question again in a way that Toshio might understand as we're now in the big grand entrance hall of the school and there is an

AWFUL din coming from somewhere.

"AAAARRRRGGHHH!"

I quickly glance at the elegant staircase wending up to the first floor – it's empty of children, goats and screamers.

Glancing the other way, I see light spilling in through the open double doors of the front entrance. Lulu is standing there with her back to us talking to a smartly dressed couple. None of them appear to be screaming.

"AAAARRRRGGHHH!"

OK, so it's coming from a doorway along the corridor directly ahead of us.

"AAAARRRRGGHHH!"

Is someone being murdered in the dining room?

"Stay still, dear!" I hear Granny Viv's voice say. "It's only FLOUR, Blossom. Look, a damp cloth is taking it all off. See?"

"Sorry about that!" we now hear Lulu say perkily to the smart couple. "One of the other girls from Newts Class mentioned that our very own superhero got half the cupcake ingredients over her costume and is a bit upset about it!"

Me, Swan and Zed turn our heads like meerkats so that we can have a nosy at whoever Lulu is talking to. Toshio isn't very curious – he just puts his headphones on and wanders back towards the reception. I suppose he's already met the couple hovering out there and just fancies getting back to his ~~music and computer games~~ work.

I pad a little closer to the front entrance, and see that the man Lulu is talking to has a fizzy cloud of black hair arranged around a big, shiny bald spot and the woman has the sort of expression someone might have if you were waving a week-old dead fish under their nose.

"But anyway, you two go right ahead and enjoy your concert tour," Lulu switches to saying, since the snooty-looking couple on the steps aren't smiling at her jokey comment about Blossom. "Don't worry about your little miss – we'll take good care of her."

"Oh, but we won't worry," says the woman as the man nods in agreement. "Our daughter is very intelligent and we've brought her up to be totally independent. She'll be absolutely fine, we have no doubt."

Me, Swan and Zed swap our puzzled frowns for quizzical glances.

"Another student?" Zed says in a whisper.

"Guess so," Swan replies. "Hey, you're not going to be the new girl any more, Dani Dexter!"

I blink back at Swan and grin. The school is **expanding**. With a new girl, that brings the total of students here at St Grizzle's to a mighty twenty-one!

"Well, we'd better go or we'll miss our flight," says the man matter-of-factly. "It leaves in... Oh, my! There's a goat on the roof of our car!"

"Ah, it's only Twinkle. Toot your horn when you get in and she'll jump off," Lulu tells the couple brightly as they edge warily towards the chunky black car parked in the driveway.

Twinkle looks quite settled on the roof, nibbling delicately at the aerial.

"Bye!" Lulu calls out and waves, then turns

round with a beaming Cheshire-cat grin on her face. "Oh, hello, you lot!"

"What's going on, Mum?" asks Zed.

Lulu looks so happy I wonder if she might break out into a tap dance of joy.

No wonder – the previous version of St Grizelda's had a ton of students but as soon as Lulu changed the style of the place from old-fashioned-and-stiff to mega-fun-and-cool, nearly all the parents flipped out and moved their girls to other schools.

If a pupil is COMING instead of GOING it's got to be a very pleasant surprise for her.

"Follow me – I've got someone I want you to meet!" says Lulu as she leads the way towards her office, along the corridor and past the dining room. (I peek in and see Super-Grrrl standing with her arms crossed, moody lip stuck out, as Granny Viv pulls a funny face and tries to cheer her up.)

"So that's what your Very Important Meeting was about today? Why didn't you tell us?" Swan asks her mum, looking extremely huffy with Lulu for keeping the arrival of the new girl a secret.

"Darling, I didn't even know we'd end up with another student today!" Lulu grins over her shoulder. "I thought Mr and Mrs Featherton-Snipe were just coming for a chat and to check out the school. I had no idea they'd liked the look of the new brochure so much that they planned to drop off their daughter with us, just like that! But here is the lovely –" Lulu hurries into her office, arms wide – "Boudicca!"

Boo-dick-ah.

Boo!

BOO!

So THAT's what Toshio had been trying and failing to say just now.

I can't blame him for finding the name tricky.

I've heard the name Boudicca before but that's cos we did a lesson about her at my old school. We found out she was a **fierce British warrior queen** from a zillion years ago. If Toshio tried to get me to say the name of some **fierce Japanese empress** from a zillion years ago, I bet I'd end up with my tongue in a knot.

But anyway, here is THIS Boudicca.

And THIS Boudicca is a very small girl who's completely sunk into one of the two huge, squashy beanbags in Lulu's office. She has a waterfall of long wavy hair that goes on forever and skinny, knobbly knees.

She does not look much like a warrior queen.
She looks more like a kid who is wondering why...

a) the head teacher has beanbags instead of
proper chairs

b) there are spray-painted toucans and
flamingos on the wall, and...

c) there's a big, snoring dog in the OTHER
beanbag.

(The answer to those questions are: Lulu
thinks it's more relaxing; Swan spray-painted
them, and Downboy is **my** dog – he and Granny
Viv turned up at St Grizzle's to check up on me
a week or so ago and never left.)

"Boudicca is eight so she'll be in Newts Class,"
Lulu tells us. "And Boudicca, this is Swan, Zed and
Dani, who are the oldest students at St
Grizelda's. They're in Fungi Class."

Boudicca stares at us with large blank grey
eyes as we smile and wave hello at her. By her

side is a suitcase that's practically bigger than she is as well as what appears to be a violin case.

"They'll keep an eye out for you," Lulu says cheerfully, trying to break the awkward silence. "Won't you, guys?"

"Um, yeah!" I hurriedly say.

"Uh-huh!" Swan agrees with a shrug of her shoulders.

"Definitely!" Zed chips in.

Boudicca stares some more at us and seems to sink deeper into the beanbag like it's a gloop of quicksand swallowing her up.

"So... I thought we could have a nice getting-to-know-everyone session in the hall before lunch," says Lulu, holding a hand out to the new girl to help her escape from her seat. "But how about you three quickly show Boudicca the school while I round everyone up? You can leave the case here for now."

"Sure," I answer as Boudicca begins to walk silently towards us, staring, staring with those big blank eyes.

You know, she sort of reminds me of someone but I can't think who.

"And Boudicca," Lulu calls after us, "I can promise you that you are going to have SUCH fun here at St Grizelda's!"

Boudicca doesn't smile or respond. She just follows me, Swan and Zed along the corridor, staring straight ahead.

"I know it's hard leaving your parents," I say in my best friendly voice, thinking that this small, knobbly kneed girl with her curtains of hair is probably just frozen with shyness and sadness. "But you'll settle in soon. I haven't been here that long and I love it. Cos like Lulu says, it's a lot of fun at St Grizzle's."

Boudicca looks straight up at me with an

expression that's hard to read – but it doesn't seem particularly shy or sad.

Hmm. Something tells me that looking after this strange girl is going to be the OPPOSITE of fun. A bit more like, like...

"AAAARRRRGGHHH!"

Blossom roars from somewhere close by.

Exactly, I think to myself...

Chapter 3
Getting To Know You... Or Not

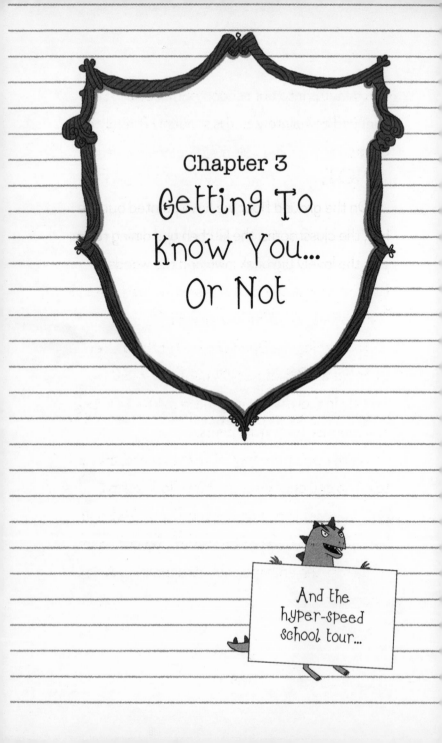

And the hyper-speed school tour...

Ten minutes into our school tour Boudicca has changed completely, and is suddenly friendly and chatty.

NOT.

On the ground floor we have pointed out the hall, the classrooms, the kitchen and dining room, plus the lovely big back lawn and the woods beyond, as well as Zed's own private room near Lulu's office, which he shares with Twinkle.

The whole time Boudicca said nothing, even when we walked into Zed's room and found Twinkle in there with her head in a drawer, eating his favourite Star Wars pants.

We're now at the foot of the staircase, about to go up and check out the first-floor dorms.

"OK, sorry I can't do this part!" says Zed, and before we can respond he spins round and zooms off across the entrance hall, disappearing down a corridor.

Here are some facts about Zed – he is...

· funny and kind and a bit shy

· very good at juggling

· great at helping the younger Grizzlers with their homework

· able to do impressive wheelies

· always cheerful and only ever gets the TINIEST bit fed up when his wheelchair stops him from doing stuff like wandering through the woods at the back of the school (too many tricksy tree roots) or hanging out upstairs in the dorms with the rest of us (too many tricksy steps and no lift).

But right now Zed doesn't seem at all bothered about being stranded on the ground floor and missing out on the chance to be a guide for the rest of

Boudicca's tour. He's properly relieved – and I don't blame him. I hadn't realized how tiring it can be to have a one-sided conversation. Swan's getting stressed out with the strain of it, too – she's blowing and **POP!**ing her bubblegum at hyper-speed.

Speaking of hyper-speed...

"Come on," I try to say cheerfully, and hurry up the stairs two at a time. We need to get this awkwardness over with as quickly as possible, before I run out of words or **Swan POPS!** too fast and ends up with a bubblegum face mask.

Luckily Swan seems to read my mind and matches me step for step. As for our newbie Newt – she's right on our heels.

"So THIS is Conkers' dorm," Swan announces, practically galloping to the first room she comes to on the left of the landing.

She throws open the door, and Boudicca peers

around at the big room that belongs to Yas, Klara, Angel and May-Belle. Like all the dorms it's got a ton of spare beds in it from when St Grizzle's was awash with pupils. Still, NOT sharing with very many people means the girls of Conkers have plenty of wall space to decorate. All around loom posters of Taylor Swift, unicorns, Bollywood film stars and Goth bands called things like Gloom and Blahhh (the Conkers have VERY different tastes).

Boudicca says nothing.

Then we go to the next room.

"This is Otters' dorm," I announce.

In among the empty beds Boudicca surveys the three that are lined up together with three identical star-patterned duvets and three identical photos of the triplets' smiley parents on each of their bedside tables.

Boudicca says nothing.

"This way to YOUR dorm," says Swan, zipping to the far end of the corridor in the opposite direction.

The door she stops at this time is covered with messy, smeared prints of twenty hands that've been dipped in different-coloured paint. Above it is a graffit'd sign:

Newts burrow here.
Death to Introoders!!

I glance at Boudicca to see what she makes of it but of course it's impossible to tell. It's also impossible to guess what she's thinking when she sees inside… The Newts' dorm is the usual disaster with its carpet of dirty socks, old loom bands, twigs, leaves, half-made craft projects, feathers and sweet wrappers.

"I know it's pretty messy but to be fair to the Newts no one knew you were coming today," says Swan. "We'll get the girls to tidy it up."

"And, hey – why don't you have the bed in the corner?" I add, looking past all the spare beds that are piled HIGH with random bobbins. "No one sleeps in that one!"

You BET no one sleeps there. The bed I'm pointing to is currently a den of sheets and towels, held together with clothes pegs, with a home-made pirate flag drawn on a bit of cardboard and tied to a skinny long tree branch with raggedy string.

Boudicca says nothing.

Sigh

I mean, I know the triplets of Otter class can be a bit silent and weird but they do giggle – a **lot** – which shows they're human at least. So far Boudicca seems to have less personality than the statue of St Grizelda, standing serenely on her plinth outside...

POP! goes yet another pink bubble of gum and Swan nods her head in the direction of the door across the hall.

"OK, last on the tour is our room – me and Dani's," she tells Boudicca, ushering her to follow us.

Swan is already rattling her key in the door of our dorm. I have a key, too ... it's the only way to stop the Newts from invading and using our place for one of the slightly dangerous games they've invented like Top Bunk Trampolining or Hide-and-Seek-and-Everyone-Pile-on-Top-Yelling.

As Boudicca silently shuffles in I'm expecting a whole lot more nothing even though I have the most amazing giant mural of a T rex on the wall next to my bed, painted for me as a welcome-to-St-Grizzle's present by Swan. (Well, technically it was more of a welcome-to-St-Grizzle's-and-sorry-I-wasn't-very-friendly-at-first present as WELL as being a sorry-I-let-Twinkle-chew-your-toy-T-rex pressie...)

Sure enough Boudicca just blinks a bit at the mural and turns away as if seeing humongous dinosaurs was the dullest thing EVER.

Then her grey-eyed stare spots Swan's flock of colourful birds on the wall around her top bunk. I swear there're more and more birds there every time I look.

"I like them."

"You what?" says Swan, bending down closer to Boudicca.

But before Boudicca can repeat her tiny, whispered comment there's a mad pattering of feet outside in the corridor.

Blossom LOLLOPS into the room, launches into a spirited twirl on the spot and then stops, suddenly and wobbily, striking what I THINK is supposed to be a superhero pose.

"Yes? Can we help you?" I ask, glad to see Super-Grrrl is looking a lot less "AAAARRRRGGHHH!" than she was earlier. From the telltale crumbs around her mouth, I suspect Granny Viv has bribed Blossom into cheerfulness with the aid of cupcakes.

In fact Blossom's holding a cupcake in one of her hands.

"Lulu says can you come to the hall NOW cos we're all there," says Blossom, relaxing her pose. "And HERE, this is for YOU!"

Blossom holds out the cupcake to Boudicca, who stares at it as if someone has offered her a worm sandwich. Maybe it's because it's technically only HALF a cupcake with the obvious half-moon of a bite mark spoiling the gift a little.

"No, thank you," mutters Boudicca in a whispered mouse-squeak, taking a step back in disgust, I suppose, though her face is as blank as usual.

Blossom gulps, and looks worryingly as if she might cry at the rejection of her gift. She might be part-goblin but she is also part-sweetheart…

"Maybe Boudicca's eaten on the way here and isn't hungry," I jump in and say quickly. "But I'll have it!"

Blossom brightens up immediately and hands me the half-a-cupcake.

"Look, I decorated it with a pretty LEAF!" she says proudly.

"Mmm!" I mumble, wishing it was an icing-sugar leaf rather than one from the garden that comes with its own ANT. "I'll, um, just leave it on my bedside table for later…"

"Right, come on," Swan says sharply, "everyone's waiting for us downstairs." With that she shoos us all out of the dorm and locks up behind us. As we head for the stairs I spot Boudicca gazing up at the curl of steps that sweep up to the top floor.

"Miss Amethyst and Mademoiselle Fabienne and my Granny Viv have rooms up there," I tell her.

"Yeah, and in the olden days before this was a school that would have been the servants' quarters," Swan adds as she catches up with us. "It's why the rooms up there are smaller and cosier than the rest of the building."

"There are PRISON CELLS up there, too!" says Blossom, eyes wide with excitement.

"I've told you before, they're just old storage cupboards," Swan says wearily. "Servants would have kept things in there like bedding and towels and candlesticks and—"

"PRISONERS!" Blossom bursts in gleefully as she hurtles off down the stairs.

Boudicca doesn't move.

She's still staring up the curl of steps. And now I see what she's staring at...

OK, so she wasn't at ALL interested in a description of the second floor. She'd been staring at Downboy, stretched out across the whole width of a polished wooden stair, snoring gently.

"Is that another dog?"

"What? No – it's the same one you met in Lulu's room. He just sort of roams around, like Twinkle," I tell her. "Here, Downboy – come and say hello to Boudicca!"

At the mention of his name, Downboy wakes up, jumps to his feet and skitters down the stairs to meet us.

Uh-oh, that was the wrong thing to do – Boudicca backs away as soon as he gets within patting distance.

"I don't like dogs. Animals are dirty. They have germs."

I look at my darling Downboy and feel a little bit offended. How can anyone not love that dopey, smiley face? And he certainly ISN'T dirty. Not compared to the Newts, anyway...

"Humans have germs, too. And some germs – like bacteria – can be healthy to have," says Swan, putting a hand on Boudicca's back and directing her down the stairs. "You'll learn stuff like that in science class with Miss Amethyst."

I follow behind, still smarting from the doggy insult. Downboy stays where he is, happily scratching behind his ear. (I hope he doesn't have fleas again.)

"There you are! Come on in and join us!" I hear Lulu call out as we finally approach the hall.

Oh! Everyone – students AND staff – are sitting in a circle on the floor. Except for Zed, that is, who is in his chair, holding a ball decorated with a smiley blue blobby fish.

"Come on, everyone, make space for Dani, Swan and Boudicca," Lulu cheerfully orders.

The triplets kindly scrunch up, giving us plenty of room. Even so, Blossom leaves as big a gap as she can manage between herself and the new girl. I think she's still hurt by Boudicca's reaction to her thoughtful gift.

"So, we're going to play a getting-to-know-each-other game," says Lulu. "Here's how it works… when the *Finding Dory* ball comes your way, you say your name and tell us all something interesting about yourself. Then it's your turn to roll the ball to someone else. Got it? Zed – will you start us off?"

Zed nods, looking proud of the responsibility, and says, "I'm Zed Chen-Murphy and I can touch my nose with my tongue."

I'm very impressed, especially by how much his eyes cross when he does it. In fact everyone's very impressed and gives him a round of applause, all except for Boudicca.

Beaming, Zed seems to forget for a second to roll the ball.

In that moment I realize that although this exercise is for Boudicca's benefit, it's going to be very useful to me, too. The Conkers I'm cool with – I hang out quite a lot with Angel, Klara, Yas and May-Belle.

But the Newts... I've heard all ten of their names around school but I can never tell them apart (except for Blossom) as they usually move about in a very fast, very mud-streaked **blur**.

As for the triplets, I only just found out their names at the weekend when I came across Granny Viv sewing nametags in their identical clothes: "Tia", "Tiane" and "Tineesha". Swan says the names are so similar that no one ever uses them. Including the triplets.

But here in the circle, I will concentrate **hard** and try and learn which Newt and Otter is which while the ball rolls back and forth and... Oh, Zed has suddenly remembered what to do with the ball and Dory is now rolling head-over-tail towards ME.

"Um, I'm Dani Dexter..." I mumble as I catch it, then stop.

What should I say for my interesting thing?

That my mum is a zoologist working in the South Pole?

Or that Granny Viv is wonderful and mad and ended up here at St Grizzle's because she was SPYING on me, till Lulu caught her and ended up asking her to stay?

Or should I say that I am really, really good at making mini-movies and helped the school win a short film competition last week?

Gulp

The last half hour I've been SO busy looking after strange little Boudicca that Arch went temporarily out of my mind. But mentioning mini-movies suddenly makes me picture his adorably goofy grin. A knot of worry tightens in my tummy and my eyes go all prickly. Before anyone notices them watering I blink, blink, blink and **blurt** out the first thing that comes into my mind.

"...and I'm glad I'm not the new girl any more,"

I say quickly, and deliberately roll the ball towards Boudicca.

Boudicca, sitting cross-legged with her hands neatly in her lap, stares at the blue fishy ball as it gently rolls towards her ... and carries ON staring as it rolls straight past her – into the waiting jaws of Downboy.

Boudicca jerks when she sees him so close like he's a giant dog-shaped flu bug.

As for Downboy, he immediately thunders from the room with his prize.

Out in the corridor, there's a loud protesting "Meh!", which I'm guessing means Twinkle has just spotted Downboy's loot. A clatter of many claws and deep growls and Meh!-ing follows as a furry battle rages for possession of Dory...

"Well, **that** was fun!" says Lulu, trying to sound positive, even though the getting-to-know-each-other session has been a big flop and lasted precisely one and a half minutes. "Er, shall we have lunch early?"

At the mention of food, everyone cheers and jumps to their feet.

Except Boudicca, who stays in her cross-legged position, watching silently as everyone files out.

And except me, too, since my mobile has just vibrated in my pocket.

Is it Arch??

At LAST???

Chapter 4
The Super-Geek Brainiac of St Grizzle's Award

And Mum's "missing you" poem...

'South Pole Poem'

Every morning I wake up
And can't believe I'm here,
In this paradise of frozen ice
With penguins oh so near!

The light is crystal clear,
The sky is brightest blue,
The only thing that's missing
In this wonderland is YOU!

Love and hugs, Mum xxxx

So the e-mail that pinged through when I was in the hall earlier – it WASN'T from Arch like I'd hoped.

It was from Mum, which was lovely, of course.

(She sent through a text straight after her poem, saying it took her **ages** to write since she tried at first to find things to rhyme with "penguin" and "zoologist" and got totally stuck.)

But the poem was ever so cute and made me go all kind of squishy inside. I've put my phone in the pocket on the front of my dungaree dress so that it feels like Mum is as **near** as can be to my heart.

As for Arch? I want to talk to Granny Viv about the whole silence situation, and what might be going on with him, as she's very good at giving advice. Though in the last few days since she and Downboy properly settled at St Grizzle's it's been really hard to get my gran on her own. Everyone loves her and wants to spend time with her, the teachers included. And she's SO grateful to Lulu for employing her as the cook and housekeeper while I'm here that she's given herself about five more jobs than Lulu ever asked her to do (personal assistant to Lulu, school counsellor, homework helper, bedtime storyteller, night-time tucker-inner). In fact, I've spoken to Granny Viv a whole lot less in the last week than I ever have before...

And I can see she's busy right now in the dining room, scraping and shooing kids away from the windows. I've lost count of the squashed noses, circles of steamy mouth-breath and greasy fingers that have been smearing the inside of the dining-room windows as everyone gawps out at us – or, more likely, gawps at the new girl.

We're sitting with Boudicca at the picnic table on the back lawn away from the mayhem. Lulu thought St Grizzle's latest student might be feeling overwhelmed by the hectic muddle of school, goats, dogs and Newts so she invited me, Swan, Zed and Miss Amethyst to join her and Boudicca for lunch. But if Lulu thought being out here in the sunshine in our smaller group would make the new girl more relaxed and talkative, she was wrong. Boudicca is just cutting up her quiche and potato salad into teeny-weeny squares and picking at them like a little bird, while Lulu and Miss Amethyst struggle to make small talk. With every direct question, Boudicca nods or shakes her head or sometimes gives her bony shoulders a shrug.

"Everything all right with your lunch?" (Nod)

"Would you like some more?" (Shake)

"Do you have any favourite foods?" (Shrug)

Apart from her thoughts on lunch, Lulu and Miss Amethyst have tried asking Boudicca about her parents, her favourite school subjects, if she has any hobbies, interests or pets, but it's been a bit like trying to make conversation with one of the woodlice the Otters and Conkers drew earlier.

She was even stony-faced when Zed tried to entertain her with his juggling skills, using two cherry tomatoes and a new potato.

"Right, I think it's time for the Newts' science lesson!" Miss Amethyst finally announces. "Come along, Boudicca. Follow me!"

Wordlessly, Boudicca places her fork and knife neatly on the plate and follows Miss Amethyst towards the back door of the school, passing Granny Viv coming the opposite way.

From behind, with her endlessly long hair and her spindly little legs, Boudicca looks like a mash-up of a shaggy-haired Afghan hound and a sparrow. She makes my boxer-poodle cross Downboy look almost normal.

"So –" says Swan, once Boudicca has disappeared from view – "why IS that girl so weird?"

"Nothing wrong with being weird, Swan! All the best people are!" Granny Viv says brightly as she wanders towards us, her pillar-box red space buns looking especially glorious in the sunshine.

"It's not that she's weird," says Lulu, "I think it's just that she's been brought up in a solitary way."

"What do you mean?" I ask.

Me, Swan and Zed are supposed to be having our English lesson with Lulu right now but I'm quite happy to find out more about Boudicca first.

"Well, Boudicca's father is a famous conductor and her mother is a famous cello player," explains Lulu. "And they go off and give concerts all over the world."

So far that sounds a lot like everyone *else's* parents here – doing jobs that take them away for long chunks of time. May-Belle's parents are famous American country-singers who tour all the time. Angel's parents are big music Bollywood actors in India. Klara's from Germany, and her mum and dad are super-brainy professors of something-or-other who get invited to lecture about whatever-it-is-they-know to lots of other clever people in lots of different countries...

"Anyway, Boudicca's been home-schooled by a tutor till now," Lulu carries on. "So for months the only people she'd see were her tutor and the housekeeper."

Wow, sounds awful, I think to myself, feeling all-of-a-sudden sad and sorry for Boudicca. Back home I had Mum and Downboy, and Granny Viv and Arch, and all my classmates in my old school to chat with, laugh with, entertain and lick me.

(Yes, that last one DOES refer to Downboy –
though Arch did once lick my hand when I had it
slapped over his mouth to stop him gabbing
through an episode of *Doctor Who*. Yuck...)

"Anyway," says Lulu, "her parents have
decided that now is the PERFECT time for her to
become more socialized and have friends!"

"Um ... didn't you also tell me that her tutor
got a new job and her parents were desperate to
find somewhere for her to go at short notice?"
Granny Viv says to Lulu.

"Er, yes, there was that, too," Lulu admits,
probably not too keen to dwell on the fact that
St Grizzle's was someone's last resort.

"Yeah, but Boudicca is incredibly quiet and
serious," says Zed. "Do you reckon she's OK? It
would be awful to think she's unhappy and just
hiding it really well..."

"That's very sweet of you to be concerned,

Zed," Lulu says, smiling at her son. "But Mr and Mrs Featherton-Snipe said Boudicca's always been very happy in her own company. And THEY don't seem to be very emotional people so I think perhaps they've brought up their daughter to be like that, too. They were all very matter-of-fact when they said goodbye to each other. There were no hugs or tears."

"Really?" says Granny Viv, sounding shocked at the idea of a farewell that didn't involve cuddles and crying. She automatically reaches across the table for my hand and gives it a squashy I-love-you squeeze. I give her hand an I-love-you-too squeeze right back.

"So Boudicca was home-schooled and isn't very huggy but what ELSE do you know about her?" Swan carries on, pumping her mother for information.

"Er ... let's see," Lulu says thoughtfully, and begins to count Boudicca facts on her fingers. "Mrs Featherton-Snipe says she is very academic and loves to study and do homework ... that she practises her violin for at least an hour a day ... and she gives her hair a hundred brushstrokes in the morning and at bedtime."

"Hmm. Sounds like the girl needs to get some fun into that busy schedule," grumbles Granny Viv.

"Well, we'll do our best to make sure that happens, won't we?" Lulu says brightly. "And I'm sure she'll soon relax and fit right in with the rest of the Newts..."

I feel a wriggly niggle of doubt when Lulu says that. The Newts are lovely but they're also completely loopy, like puppies that have been fed too much sherbet. How is a calm girl who's used to her own company going to deal with being in a class and a dorm full of total **bonkers**-ness?

"Oh, and I just remembered," Lulu adds. "*Mr Featherton-Snipe* told me that their family don't approve of sugar so we need to bear that in mind for the menus, Viv..."

"**TSK!**" snorts Granny Viv as if that was quite the silliest thing she'd ever heard.

"...and that her name is just Boudicca and is never to be shortened."

"**HUMPH!**" laughs Swan. "Pretty big name for such a small person when you think about it, isn't it?"

Uh-oh – as everyone chats, tsks and humphs, I suddenly spot something in the garden that shouldn't be here. Or rather **someone**.

Boudicca.

She has been gone less than five minutes but here she is, padding across the lawn towards us, her big grey eyes staring.

"Lulu..." I hiss, trying to alert my head teacher to the escaped student.

Before Lulu gets a chance to turn round, Boudicca has slithered back down on to the bench beside Granny Viv and picked up one of our English study guides lying on the table.

"Um, Boudicca," says Lulu as Boudicca speedily flicks through the pages, her eyes scanning the text. "Shouldn't you be back inside, in your science class?"

"Yoo-hoo! Don't worry!" Miss Amethyst suddenly calls out, wafting out of the back door of the school with a wave of her arms and a kerfuffled look on her face. "Boudicca is just a very clever girl and has finished her worksheet ALREADY!"

"Already?" repeats Lulu. "What are the other Newts doing?"

"Chewing their pencils and trying to understand Question 1," answers Miss Amethyst.

The two teachers exchange glances.

We have one brainiac geek in the school already and that's ten-year-old Yas, who likes to read SATS papers at bedtime for fun.

But it looks like Yas MIGHT have a rival for the Super-Geek Brainiac of St Grizzle's Award, if we actually had one!

"Why don't you come back to the classroom, Boudicca, and I'll find something else for you to do," Miss Amethyst says gently.

Without a word, without a flicker of expression on her face, Boudicca closes the book and silently trots off once again after her teacher.

"Do you think Miss Amethyst is going to struggle to find enough work for her?" Granny Viv mulls out loud.

"Do you think Boudicca understands the concept of classes since she's only ever been with a tutor?" Lulu adds to the mulling.

"Do you think she'll be back out here in another five minutes?" Zed wonders.

"Do you think she's a robot?" Swan asks, before blowing a thoughtful pink bubble of gum.

You know, I think there's a good chance Granny Viv, Lulu, Zed and Swan might ALL have a point.

Chapter 5
Night, Night...
Oops

And the home-made
name-necklaces...

Blossom
Elif
Polly
Rafaella
Giselle
Jessica
Izzy
Karima
Olive
Hana

Ten names, scribbled messily with fat felt-tip pens on rectangles of cardboard.

And all the cardboard rectangles dangle by loops of string round the necks of every Newt in the dorm.

"LOOK!" says Blossom, "we've made name-necklaces for EVERYONE!"

Sure enough the pyjama'd Newts have been very, very busy. They have not only tidied their room – possibly by sweeping all the socks and mess into the wardrobe – but they have tried to brush their hair, too, with varying degrees of success.

And, of course, they have *very thoughtfully* made a giant name-necklace for every person in the whole school to wear. Three for members of staff are on a nearby bed – Toshio and Granny Viv's get top marks for correct spelling, and Looloo is a good try, I guess. On the floor is one made out for Miss Amthist, while another is ready for Madmossle Fabinum.

There's even one each for Downboy and
Twinkle. (Good luck with THOSE lasting more
than five seconds without being eaten...)

"And this one is for YOU!" says Blossom, taking
a name-necklace out from behind her back that
reads Dani Dexterer. Hey, close enough.

A girl who is apparently Hana, according to
HER name-necklace, stands on her tiptoes and
reaches up to place a string over Swan's head.
Even upside down, Swan can see HER name-card
reads Swarm (you have never seen such a huge
eye-roll).

"We haven't done one for Boodoo... Boodicky yet," stumbles Blossom, holding up a blank piece of card, "cos we didn't know how to spell it."

"Here," I say, taking the cardboard rectangle and a marker pen from her and writing out Boudicca's name nice and neatly.

The soon-to-be wearer of this latest name-necklace is at this moment downstairs in the kitchen. Granny Viv thought that **all** Boudicca might need to relax and feel at home here is...

a) a hot chocolate

b) a slice of home-made red velvet cake, and

c) a cosy chat with a friendly grannyish person. (Though Granny Viv isn't very grannyish – she likes punk music and driving madly painted camper vans for a start.)

But knowing what we know about Boudicca so far, I think their get-together will be a lot less cosy and sugary than Granny Viv expects.

Boudicca is probably sitting at the kitchen table right now sipping a glass of lukewarm water and staring silently at Granny Viv and her bright red hair...

Anyway, while Boudicca is doing whatever she's doing with Granny Viv, me and Swan are up here inspecting the dorm and giving the Newts a little pep talk about being on their best behaviour with Boudicca.

"Remember, she isn't used to other children," I tell them. "So you have to be patient and kind, and not, er, TOO full-on."

"Full-on?" repeats Blossom, looking confused.

"Dani means don't act like the maniac goblins you really are," Swan butts in, speaking more plainly. "Not till she gets used to you, at least."

Aw... Blossom and the other maniac goblins look a teeny bit hurt, which makes me feel bad. After all they've been very sweet from what I can make out. As well as attempting to tidy the dorm and their hair, and slaving away on the name-necklaces, the girls of Newts Class have also cleared the pirate den from the spare bed and laid a little bunch of dandelions on Boudicca's pillow.

"By the way, the flowers ... that's a lovely idea!" I say quickly, trying to make up for insulting the Newts.

"I thought of that!" yelps Olive. (Wow, these name-necklaces really ARE useful.)

At the same time I walk over to the bed and quickly brush away the beetle, daddy-long-legs and baby snail that I've just spotted escaping from the string-tied bouquet.

"Well, here we are!" Granny Viv booms from the doorway as she gently nudges a silent Boudicca into the room.

Granny Viv might be smiling but she shoots me a quick, sharp look that reads, "Nope, the home-made cake and granny chat did NOT work..."

Knew it.

"Doesn't the dorm look great!" she carries on in a fake cheerful voice. "Oh, and what have you girls been up to? Are these name-cards? What a fantastic idea!"

"They're name-NECKLACES," Blossom corrects Granny Viv as she presents her and Boudicca with their personalized gifts.

Granny Viv looks delighted and puts hers on straight away.

Boudicca looks confused, and stares at the bit of cardboard and string being held out to her.

"Name-necklaces – excellent!" says Granny Viv, swiftly taking Boudicca's and popping it over her head before any feelings can be hurt.

OK, with capable Granny Viv here, it seems like a good time for me and Swan to sneak off, our work done.

Cos while Granny Viv wrangles the Newts into bed – checking first that teeth are clean and pyjamas aren't on backwards – it's time to start our own wind-down. Though, of course, since we're the oldest kids in school we don't have to go to sleep for ages. We can just hang out in our dorm and chat or read or paint birds on walls or whatever. And tonight, my whatever is sending Mum a thank-you-for-your-South-Pole-poem email and grabbing Granny Viv for a chat once she's done with tucking in the Newts, old and new.

But first me and Swan go to our dorm and get changed into our PJs (tartan shortie ones for me, silky Chinese ones for Swan). Then it's off to the girls' loos along the corridor – past my snoring, stretched-out dog – for a tandem tooth-brushing session, which turns into a GROUP teeth-scrub-a-thon, since Angel (fuchsia nightie), Klara (unicorn-patterned PJs), May-Belle (oversized black T-shirt with skull 'n' crossbones on it) and Yas (high-necked, white cotton nightdress) are already in there.

"So what do you think of the new girl?" Angel asks us as she twirls her long dark brown hair up into a messy bun.

Swan shrugs.

"I'm not sure it's going to work out with Boudicca," she says once she's rinsed her mouth of toothpaste.

"How do you mean?" asks May-Belle, frowning under her thick black fringe.

"Well, everyone gets on here really well, even though we're all different and obviously I'M the only normal one out of you lot," Swan announces, ignoring our laughs and protests. "But I'm not sure if Boudicca will ever fit in. I'm not sure she WANTS to fit in..."

"Yeah, but we have to give her a chance," I mumble as I brush. I think giving her time to settle in is fair even if so far I've found Boudicca trickier to understand than an extra-tricky Sudoku puzzle.

Swan gives another shrug in response as if to say all the chances in the world won't make a difference.

"Maybe Boudicca just needs a good night's sleep," says Yas. "I saw Granny Viv tiptoeing out of the dorm just before I came in here so

Boudicca and the Newts must've settled down."

Argh... Granny Viv has left and gone downstairs **already**, before I could nab her for a chat? She'll be having her dinner with the other teachers and Toshio now.

I know, I think as I rinse my toothbrush and stick it in the plastic holder. *I'll text her and see if she'll pop up for a chat after she's eaten...*

"Night," I say to everyone, and make my way out of the loos and back to our room, leaving Swan to follow when she's ready.

Stepping over a drooling, dreaming Downboy again, I reach the dorm and push the door open – it's never locked at this time of night when the Newts are safely, thankfully sleeping.

As soon as I slump down on my bunk, I grab my phone from the bedside cabinet where it's being guarded – along with a print out of Mum's 'South Pole' poem – by a plastic T rex with a bandaged

tail and leg. (He's one of the bunch of ex-toys
Arch and me collected to use as "actors" in our
mini-movies. T rex is still my favourite, even if he
HAS been chewed by Twinkle.)

Wait a minute...

· the poem

· my T rex

· Zed's suggestion this morning in science that
I should shoot a cool new mini-movie that'll get
Arch's attention.

WHAM! Those three thoughts crash together
and turn into a BRILLIANT idea.

Here's what I'll do – I'll mess around with the
words of Mum's poem and then shoot my T rex
"reciting" it.

Once I have another read-through it takes no
time at all to adapt.

Next I kneel by the bedside cabinet and with
one hand I point my phone at my T rex.

With the other hand, I hold his tail so I can move him as he speaks.

And THIS is what he says...

'The St Grizzle's Poem'

Every morning I wake up
And can't believe I'm here,
In this paradise of nuttiness
With crazy students oh so near!

The classes are bizarre,
The teachers bonkers too,
The only thing that's missing
In this goofy place is YOU!

I press stop.

I flip my mini-movie back to the beginning and watch it through. Happy with it, I upload it to

YouTube and smile. Now all I have to do is wait till Arch sees my film and—

"DANI!" shrieks Granny Viv, barging into the dorm closely followed by a now wide-awake Downboy.

I leap so much that my head misses banging the bunk above by about a squillimetre.

"What? What is it?" I squeak, her panic infectious.

Behind Granny Viv there's a frantic pad-padding of feet as Swan and the Conkers come scurrying out of the loos and along the corridor.

"She's gone!" Granny Viv announces, clutching her heaving chest as yet MORE girls turn up behind her. Even the sleepy-looking Otter triplets have materialized, wondering what's happening.

"Who's gone?" I ask.

"Boudicca! I just came up to check on her but when I put my head round the Newts' dorm door I saw that her bed was empty. I woke them up and had them searching under every bed and in every nook and cranny but she's not there!"

Oops. We've lost the new girl? Already?

"She's not in the girls' loos," says Swan. "We've all been in there chatting."

"Let's go check OUR dorm," Klara says to her dorm-mates, waving at them to follow her.

"I'll help the triplets check THEIR room," Yas offers.

"Can you check in here, Dani?" Granny Viv asks me.

"There's no point," I tell her. "I've been here for ages. I'd've noticed if Boudicca had come in."

"Hmm... Well, we'll have to get a search party organized," Granny Viv announces. "Swan, hurry downstairs and tell your mum and the others what's happened. The rest of you, let's check the dorms, then we'll meet up in the school hall and plan where to look next. Come on – chop, chop!"

Granny Viv claps her hands together and shoos everyone out. I try to hurry after them but get my foot tangled in my duvet and have to hop around gasping as I attempt to stop myself tumbling and breaking my fall with my face.

"Hee!"

At that tiny sound I stop dead on one leg like a startled, tartan-pyjama-wearing flamingo.

Where did it come from, that teeny-weeny hee! sound?

"ARF!"

I look round. Downboy might be fairly stupid – ninety-nine per cent stupid actually – but right now he's using his one per cent of intelligence to give me a clue.

"ARF! ARF!!"

He's at the bunk bed in the opposite corner to mine... Swan's bunk. Downboy's got his fuzzy front paws on the ladder like he's planning on climbing up to the top bunk and settling down for the night.

Only there won't be room for him up there – it's already taken. And not by Swan, who's rounding up the teachers.

Kicking myself free of the duvet, I walk towards the small mound under Swan's duvet. As I get closer I spot a pair of grey eyes peering at me.

"Boudicca?" I say. "What are you doing? Didn't

you hear Granny Viv? Everyone's looking for you. They think you're missing."

Boudicca blinks at me and bites at her lip but says nothing.

"How did you even get in here without me noticing?" I ask. "Wait a minute... Did you sneak in while me and Swan were off brushing our teeth?"

"Mmm-hmm," comes a tiny reply.

"But why didn't you stay with the other Newts?"

"They are too many. And they are too talky."

Actually, when it comes to Boudicca, too many Talky Newts does NOT equal a Happy Weird Shy-Girl.

"Look, they're just trying to be friendly," I say in the Newts' defence.

"But I don't want to have friends," I just catch
Boudicca's hard-to-hear murmurings.

With that, she flips round and faces the wall.
With one finger she begins to trace round the
nearest of Swan's bird flock.

"HOWWWWW-WHOOOOOOO!"
Downboy interrupts with a loud howl like he's
letting the whole school – and anyone within a
ten-kilometre radius – know what, or who, he's
found.

It does the trick, and a babble of voices and
thunder of feet sound as everyone who just
rushed DOWN the stairs now comes rushing UP
the stairs.

As a bundle of babbling staff and students pile
into the dorm, I back off towards my bunk so that
Lulu and Granny Viv can deal with our newest,
most reluctant student.

"Emergency over – back to bed, please!" Miss

Amethyst insists, shooing random Conkers, Otters and now wide-awake Newts from our room.

Since Swan can't exactly get to HER own bed right now, she comes to join me on mine.

"What's going on?" she whispers as we watch Lulu and Granny Viv talk kindly but earnestly with Boudicca.

"She told me that she doesn't want to have friends," I reply, thinking of what Boudicca just said to me in her teeny-tiny voice. "You were right, Swan – she doesn't WANT to fit in here."

I'm so caught up in that thought that it takes me a second to notice the vibration alert coming from my phone.

As soon as I do I see that the rumbling buzz is letting me know that there's a thumbs-up icon under my YouTube mini-movie.

Yes, yes, YES!

Arch is alive and – better still – online!

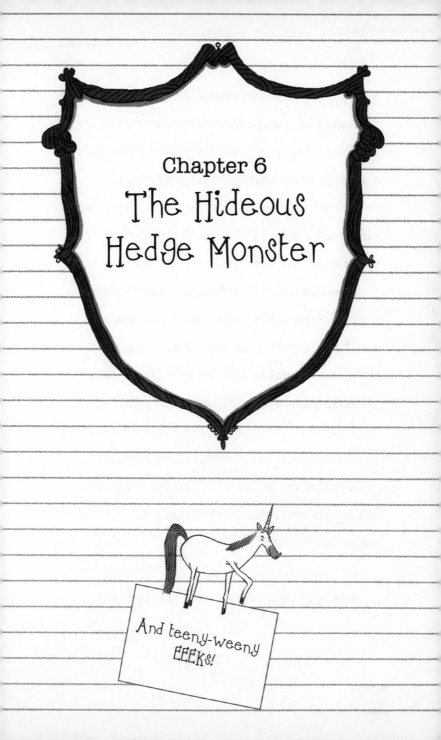

Chapter 6
The Hideous Hedge Monster

And teeny-weeny EEEKs!

Like Dr Seuss in his *Green Eggs and Ham* poem,
it seems Boudicca isn't keen on quite a LOT of
things.

She only arrived yesterday but already we all
know that...

She does not like the dorm of Newts.
She does not like the eggs Gran cooks.
She does not like the pets at school,
The students, teachers or our friendly rules.
She does not like to smile or chat.
She does not like St Grizzle's hat...

"It's silly," she said super-seriously when we
passed the statue of St Grizelda and saw the
Easter bonnet someone had tied round her stone
head this morning. Or maybe Boudicca was
referring to the fake ginger moustache that was
stuck to her upper lip. Or the blow-up rubber

swim-ring dangling round her left wrist.

But I wasn't in the mood to explain that SILLY can be GOOD.

It was because I wasn't in a very silly or good mood myself.

I'd been hoping that once Arch "liked" my poetic mini-movie last night everything would get back to normal. But no – Arch didn't leave any comments or reply to the texts I sent.

It was back to silence.

Weirdly weird, not-like-Arch-at-all silence...

I'm still mumfing about that now as I attempt to stop Downboy and Twinkle from doing a four-legged maypole dance round the lamppost outside the supermarket in the village.

As I try and untangle the knot of leads, I can see some of the kids from the local school further along the pavement. They have clipboards in their hands and sniggers on their faces. And – uh-oh

– guess who's right in the middle of the sniggerers? Meanie McMeanpants Spencer, who is saying something horrible about us right now I bet, since he is the sort of person who is allergic to niceness.

The last time we saw him was at the award ceremony the council held to announce the winner of the local schools' film project. Spencer is probably still seething about the fact that...

a) OUR film won, and

b) Granny Viv photo bombed theirs. (Go, Granny Viv, go, Granny Viv!)

"Ignore them," says Zed, who's spotted the

village kids, too. "Let's just head back to school. Are you nearly finished rearranging the shopping, Swan?"

"Almost," says his sister, placing equally weighted bags on each of the handles of Zed's wheelchair. Then she reaches inside one of the bags and grabs a few rustling somethings. "Here, catch!"

She's calling out to the triplets and Boudicca who are hovering close by, looking a little bored by our shopping trip. That's till four bags of crisps go sailing through the air towards them.

Tia, Tiane and Tineesha (proudly wearing their Newt-made cardboard name-necklaces) give matching squeals of excitement and lunge to grab at their treats.

Boudicca, holding on to an open copy of *Harry Potter and the Deathly Hallows*, watches blankly as a packet of salt 'n' vinegar lands with a flump at her feet.

We hear Spencer and his friends burst out laughing. Great.

And now he's swaggering over towards us.

"So what are these?" he asks me, Zed and Swan, pointing at the name-necklaces we're wearing. "Are you Grizzlers all so thick that you forget your own names?"

"We have a new girl. It's to help her get to know us," Zed replies in as even a voice as he can manage, while trying not to get riled by Spencer's sneer.

"Not that it's any of your business…" Swan mutters in a low growl.

"What – that little geek with all the hair?" snarls Spencer, ignoring Swan as he glances at Boudicca, who's gone back to reading her book and ignoring the rest of us.

"Lovely talking to you but we've got to go," Swan says sarcastically, picking up another couple of shopping bags.

"Hold on! Our school's doing a survey," Spencer says quickly, waving his clipboard in our faces. "Can I ask you the purpose of your visit to the village today?"

Strangely Spencer sounds almost polite when he says that last bit, which isn't normal for him. And then I get why – his teacher is striding towards us, giving him an encouraging nod.

"Is it business or pleasure?" Spencer carries on in his fake polite voice, his pencil poised over a couple of tick boxes.

The reason for us coming to the village is neither.

Since yesterday's failed science lesson and last night's failed bedtime with the Newts, Lulu has had a rethink. To keep things simple she allowed Boudicca to sleep in a spare bunk in the dorm with me and Swan in the end but told us she'd like to try moving Boudicca in with the Otters' group today. She's hopeful it'll suit Boudicca better, since...

· the schoolwork will be a little harder
· the dorm will be a little quieter, and
· the triplets are generally a little stranger, same as Boudicca.

And in an attempt to get them to bond, Lulu asked me, Swan and Zed to go and buy some groceries, taking the triplets and Boudicca with us.

But there's been no bonding. On the walk along the leafy country road to get here

Boudicca trotted along in silence, ignoring the triplets and the only-a-little-bit-stale marshmallows they offered her. When the triplets started playing tag in the freezer aisles of the supermarket just now, Boudicca parked herself by the cat litter and buried herself in the book she'd brought along.

"Business or pleasure," Spencer repeats loudly, before adding under his breath. "Or just taking your pet dorks for a walk?"

He nods his head in the direction of Boudicca and the triplets.

You know, I'd quite like to grab his pencil and scribble GO AWAY! in big letters all over his stupid survey. But while Spencer might be as pleasant as a shark with bad breath, we have to keep our temper and uphold the reputation of St Grizzle's in front of his approaching teacher.

"Well, hello! Everything fine here?" the teacher

asks brightly.

"Absolutely brilliant, thanks," says Swan, slapping a smile on her face that's as fake as Spencer's politeness. "But we're expected back at school soon, so bye!"

Following her lead, me and Zed make our escape, hustling the crisp-eating triplets and the book-reading Boudicca ahead of us, dragging Downboy and Twinkle after us.

"Hey, I haven't finished yet!" Spencer calls out.

"Tough," Swan mutters under her breath as she reaches out and JUST manages to grab book-reading Boudicca before she and Harry Potter walk straight into the bus stop...

"So what happens if you-know-who DOESN'T fit in at St Grizzle's?" Zed asks quietly on the journey home along the country road.

The triplets are skipping on ahead in single-file togetherness while Boudicca trundles behind us, blinking her big grey unreadable eyes whenever one of us checks on her and asks if she's all right.

"I guess Lulu tells her parents it's not working and they find her another tutor," says Swan.

That suddenly makes me feel another wrench of sorry and sad for Boudicca. Being stuck at home with just a tutor and some housekeeper for company while her parents are off touring ... it doesn't seem like a shy girl's dream to me – it sounds properly LONELY.

Suddenly I can't bear to think of little Boudicca going back to that odd, friendless life.

I should try harder to help her to settle in. I told the Newts last night that they had to be patient with her. I mean, I didn't much like St Grizzle's when I first arrived. The trouble was I was so MAD at Mum for sending me there that I couldn't see how fantastic it was.

Perhaps, in her own way, Boudicca is cross with *her* parents.

Perhaps, perhaps, perhaps it'll take quite a while for St Grizzle's and its goofy charms to win over this strange girl...

I turn to check on her again – and suddenly see that Boudicca has frozen. She's standing stock-still, her eyes staring straight at me.

For the first time she has an expression I understand: ALARM.

I'm about to ask, "What? What's wrong?" when I hear The Thing that's caught her attention.

Actually, we've ALL come to a stop as a strange collection of noises come from behind the hedge on the other side of the quiet road.

There's a lot of scrabbling.

Rustles and crackles.

A sort of panting sigh.

By the time I hear a growling, gasping cry, my heart is thudda-dudda-dudding in alarm.

"**ARF! ARF! ARF!**" goes Downboy, yanking hard on his lead.

Glancing round at Zed, Swan and the triplets, I can tell we're all a nanosecond away from one of us yelling, "Run!"

But then Boudicca makes a surprisingly dramatic sound for her.

"EEEEEEEK!"

She points and we stare.

Stare at a **WILD-EYED MONSTER** emerging from the hedge!

OK, so it's more of a **WILD-EYED PERSON**.

A **WILD-EYED BOY**, actually.

The wild-eyed boy locks eyes with me for a second before my dog pulls the lead from my hand and rushes over to POUNCE on him.

"Woah! Ha! Get down, Downboy," laughs a voice I know so well.

And before I know it, I'm running over to pounce on Arch, too...

Chapter 7
The Unexpected Guest

And some sads and happys...

"But WHY are you here?" I ask Arch as we pass the sign for "**St Grizelda's School for Girls**" and turn into the school's drive. The smart "**Grizelda**" part of the sign has a spray-painted line through it and a hand-squiggled "**Grizzle's**" added above.

Arch is in too much pain to notice. He's limping – he climbed over a stile in a fence on his way here and the rotten wood gave way under him, leaving him with a bruised and scraped knee.

As for Swan and the others, they're up ahead of us, and just now I overheard Swan phoning Lulu to tell her to expect an unexpected guest.

Well, not EVERYONE is up ahead of us. Boudicca is tagging along by Arch's side, making herself useful by holding his backpack, which he dropped when he blundered out of the hedge. She keeps gazing up at him as if he is a famous pop star or something instead of a dishevelled eleven-year-old boy who shouldn't be here.

"I'm here cos of the film you posted last night." Arch answers my question, leaning on my shoulder for support. "You said in your poem that all that was missing at St Grizzle's was ME. So I thought I'd better pay you a visit!"

As ever Arch is trying to sound jokey. But him turning up like this – truanting from school on a Thursday, travelling all the way here on his own ... it's not really funny ha-ha stuff, I think, as a pancake-of-worry flips in my tummy.

And no wonder we mistook Arch for a wild-eyed monster – he looks like he's been dragged through a hedge backwards. Which he pretty much has – it took both me and Swan to pull him free of the thorny branches back when he made his surprise appearance.

"So how did you get here?" I ask, remembering the long, long drive from home on the day Mum dropped me off at St Grizzle's.

"Well, I worked out I needed to take three buses and that was fine – till I jumped off at the wrong stop. I ended up using the map on my phone to go cross-country," he says in a bright and breezy voice as if it was all a bit of a lark.

I glance at my friend as he talks – he has twigs and leaves of several different species of tree attached to his hair and clothes, plus cheeks smeared green with grass and criss-crossed with vivid pink scratches.

"That was fine, too," he continues, "till I had to take a detour through a marsh – thanks to being chased by a grumpy cow…"

Arch nods down at his supposed-to-be-white trainers, which are now a fetching shade of sludge brown, with socks to match.

And just like the photo of Arch at the lido last summer, he looks odd.

"Hey, what happened to your baseball cap?" I ask.

"I dunno... I think I might have lost it when I fell off a stile. Or maybe it was when I was running away from the mad cow or when I squeezed through the hedge."

However he lost it, without his hat, Arch's skinny face seems skinnier, his nose a little pointier, his flip of fair hair a little floppier as it falls into his eyes.

"Arch..." I begin, my tummy-pancake-of-worry flip-flapping madly as a thought suddenly strikes me. "Do your mum and dad know you're here?"

I'm not sure what I'm expecting Arch to say. Maybe he'll make another jokey comment? Give me an excuse? Tell me a lie? Cos something is

117

just **not** right.

But I'm kind of knocked sideways when all of a sudden, my funny, easy-going friend begins to cry...

He's still sobbing silent, snotty, hiccupping tears when Granny Viv runs down the driveway to meet us.

"Hello, Arch!" she says warmly as if she'd been expecting him. "Here, let me give you a hand." And she puts her arm round his waist so we can BOTH help him hip-hop inside the school.

He's still crying in that can't-quite-get the-words-out way when Granny Viv plonks him on a beanbag in Lulu's office. I pull the other one as close as I can and sink down into it.

"There, there ... take slow, deep breaths," says Lulu, kneeling down beside Arch and rubbing comforting circles on his back.

"I'm going to pop and get the first-aid kit so we can get you cleaned up," Granny Viv says from the office doorway, but I know that's code for "AND I'm off to call Arch's parents".

I'm glad. Although it's brilliant to see my best friend, I'm feeling MORE than a little freaked out. I mean, even without the collapsing bits of fence and stampeding cattle, Arch has put himself in real danger by taking off on his own, without anyone knowing.

And of course someone from the office at my old school must have called his parents by now, to ask why he's absent. They must be going out of their minds with worry...

"Now then, Arch," Lulu begins in a voice as soft as fluffy clouds. "I'm Lulu, the head teacher here. I've heard SO much about you, and seen a lot of the great films you and Dani have made together!"

I don't know whether it's the calming back rub or hearing the nice compliment but Arch manages to look up at Lulu and give her a watery almost-smile.

"I think my favourite one has to be the giraffe Beanie Boo singing 'Somewhere Over the Rainbow' to the audience of assorted dinosaurs," she carries on. "Very moving. Nice touch to have a tissue in the claws of the brontosaurus."

"Velociraptor," Arch corrects her as he sniffily wipes away his tears with the back of his hand.

"Ah, yes, silly me. Of course it was a

velociraptor!" Lulu says with an easy laugh.
"Anyway, Arch. It really is a treat to meet you.
But what exactly has brought you here? I'm
guessing it's more than just a sudden fancy to
catch up with Dani?"

At her gentle probing, Arch's eyes fill up like
miniature paddling pools.

"I HAD to see her. I had to tell her... I..."

"What? What's wrong, Arch?" I ask as a choke
blocks the words in my friend's throat.

"It's... It's Mum and Dad, Dani," he says, after a
moment and a deep breath. "They're splitting up.
They told me at the weekend..."

No!

WHAT?

Mr and Mrs Kaminski, who I've known ever
since I was weeny, are getting **divorced**?!

But suddenly it all starts to make sense –
THAT'S why Mr and Mrs Kaminiski have been

sounding so sad and weird whenever I've phoned Arch at home recently. It was nothing to do with them feeling sorry for me being stuck in boarding school ... it was all to do with the two of them falling out of love and dreading telling their son.

And of course once they'd broken the news to Arch – well, THAT'S why he'd been out of contact the last few days.

Oh, poor Arch...

His shoulders are shaking as sobs take hold of him again.

I try to squidge closer to give him a cuddle but beanbags are notoriously hard to move in and I'm only halfway to a hug when I see a small hairy blur run over from the corner of the room.

Boudicca – she must have hunkered down there without me, Granny Viv or Lulu noticing.

"Here," she says, passing Arch a crumpled ball of already-used tissue.

"Thanks," he mutters, taking it from her. "Sorry for, you know, crying and everything. The last few days ... sometimes I've been **so** angry I can't cry and sometimes I've been **so** upset I can't stop."

"I wish I could've been around when you found out," I tell him.

"Me, too," says Arch, parping his nose. "It's been horrible at school, having no one close to talk to. And when I've got upset a couple of times, some of the kids just stared at me like I had a luminous alien fish-head or something."

Just then, Boudicca puts a hand out and begins to do something bizarre – she strokes the flop of fair hair hanging over Arch's forehead.

"You don't look like a fish," she reassures him.

Now Arch looks confused as well as upset – he's staring at this small stranger with a frown that seems to say "Who?", "Why?", "What?".

"What a kind girl you are," says Lulu. Quickly

getting to her feet, she takes the hand doing the stroking and swiftly leads Boudicca out of the office. "How about you get your violin and play something soothing out in the hall? I don't think I've heard you do any practising since you've been here. That would be nice, wouldn't it?"

"No, I don't want to," I hear Boudicca grumble as she's led away.

"Ah, well, let's see if we can find you something else to do then..." Lulu's voice drifts off down the corridor.

"Which kid is she?" Arch asks as he blows his nose.

"She's a new girl," I tell him. "She started yesterday – which I'd have told you about if you'd answered ANY of my messages!"

My teasing is rewarded with a wobbly grin.

"OK, let's get out of here and go somewhere private to talk," I suggest. "The tree house is good

– it'll just be me and you. And maybe Granny Viv, if she needs to fix your scratches. And Twinkle will probably be up there. And I bet Downboy will follow us. Some of the Newts might try and sneak up, too, but I'll send them away."

"But apart from that, we'll be totally alone." Arch grins in a less wobbly way.

"Totally," I assure him.

Then we both try and wriggle and squiggle our way out of the rustling beanbags – and fail miserably cos in the squashy circumstances we just can't help sniggering.

Arch might have turned up at St Grizzle's for a totally SAD reason but right now I feel totally HAPPY to have my best friend here…

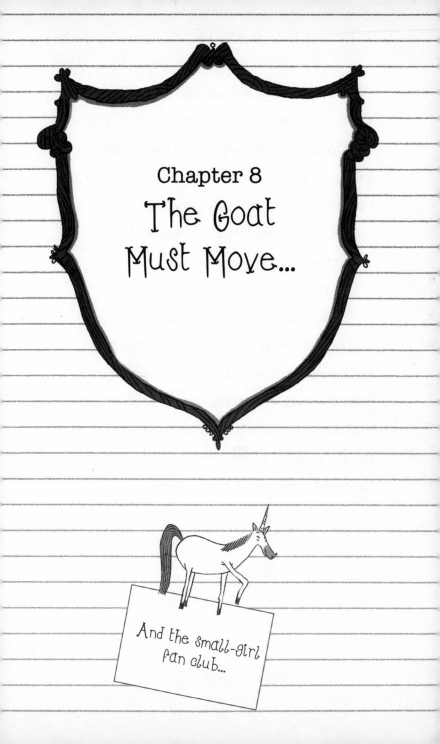

Chapter 8
The Goat
Must Move...

And the small-girl
fan club...

"Are you staying for a while?"

"Can you help us make a film?"

"Do you want to see how many cartwheels I can do in a row?"

"What's your favourite pudding?"

"Would you like to have MY pudding?"

"Can you sign this bit of paper?"

"Can you sign my arm?"

"Can you sign my FOREHEAD?"

Granny Viv has been trying to shoo all the girls away from Arch but pretty much failing.

It's like a celebrity has landed in the dining room this lunchtime, and they've all gone starry-eyed and giddy. Especially Boudicca, who's been staring at him in what looks an awful lot like wonder.

"No he's not... He won't have time... Don't do cartwheels inside or you'll knock something – or some**one** – over... No thank you, Arch has pudding of his own… He isn't going to sign that scrap of paper… OR your arm… And he definitely isn't signing your forehead, Blossom!" Granny Viv skilfully answers the scattershot of questions aimed Arch's way.

But I think Arch has kind of enjoyed the attention and it's certainly taken his mind off the fact that his parents are due here any minute. Mind you, his fingers are squeezing mine so tightly under the table that I know he's suffering from a bit of tummy-pancake-flipping of his own right now.

"OK, that's enough!" Granny Viv calls out, banging two metal lunch trays together like out-of-tune cymbals. "Everybody, back to your tables and finish your lunch!"

With a groan of disappointed "awww!"s, the various Newts, Otters and Conkers and Boudicca slouch away, leaving me, Arch, Zed and Swan alone.

"You should charge them for autographs before you go, Arch," Swan jokes in her usual dry, sarky way. "You'd make a fortune!"

"Yeah, and you'd make even MORE for a selfie!" Zed joins in. "Wouldn't he, Dani?"

"Yeah, ha!" I laugh, then wonder why Arch suddenly isn't.

All he's managed is a half-hearted smile. He's not even looking at Swan and Zed – his gaze has dropped to the half-finished red velvet cake and dollop of gloopy ice cream in his bowl.

Uh-oh, is he thinking about his parents and worried he might cry again?

"OK?" I mumble to Arch.

"Mmm," he mumbles back.

"Hello? Hello, Dani?" I suddenly hear Toshio call out from the doorway of the dining room. "Your friend – he can come now, please!"

"Your parents must be here..." I say, giving Arch's fingers an extra-tight squeeze. "Go on – it'll be OK. Your mum and dad are lovely."

With a deep, nervous gulp of air, Arch gets up, and follows Toshio as he smiles and waves for Arch to follow.

"Do you think his parents will go crazy at him?" Zed asks me.

"I think they'll just want to give him a big hug," I say, staring over the heads of the various chatting, eating, yelling girls in the hope that I can catch a glimpse of Mr and Mrs Kaminski heading to Lulu's office.

"Anyway, Arch's parents might be feeling too guilty to be mad at him," Swan points out. "You know, them splitting up making him so unhappy that he runs away?"

Before lunch, Granny Viv took Arch off to fix up his knee, giving me time to tell Swan and Zed his sad news.

"Yeah, maybe," I agree.

As I speak, I feel a tug at my leg under the table. I move my leg away, my thoughts too lost in Arch and the meet-up that's about to happen in the room just down the corridor.

"Right, I'm done," says Swan, standing up and piling her empty plates on one of the trays that Granny Viv was using as cymbals just now. "Coming, you two? We're on wash-up duty..."

"Sure," says Zed, balancing his plates on his lap and manoeuvring off.

"I'll be there in a sec – just finishing this," I say, pointing to the bowl in front of me which might be full or empty, I'm not sure. Like Arch, I haven't had much of an appetite this lunchtime.

But just as I dip my spoon in, THERE goes that tugging at my leg again.

"Stop it! Go away!" I say, bending right over and gazing under the table, expecting to find a furry someone under there.

But it's not Downboy. And it isn't Twinkle either. It's Boudicca. And she's saying something.

Only I can't hear a word of her mouse-squeak, so – with a sigh – I slide under the table to join her.

"What are you doing under here?" I ask her.

"It's too busy and loud out there," she says, pointing to the room in general. "So is the boy going to stay?"

"No," I answer her, realizing that's what the mouse-squeak was all about. "His parents are having a chat with him and Lulu but they'll be taking him home."

Boudicca looks as crestfallen as I feel.

What is it about Arch that she likes so much, so quickly, I wonder? I almost feel a tiny bit jealous. What does he have that me and Swan and Zed and the others don't?

"Look, how about I find you a seat with the triplets?" I suggest. "You'll be doing your lessons with them this afternoon and moving into the Otters' dorm tonight."

Boudicca shakes her head.

As for MY head, I crack it on the underside of the table as I try and find a more comfortable position. We can't stay here or I'll get concussion.

"Well, come with me to the kitchen and help me, Zed and Swan do the dishes instead. At least it'll be quieter in there..."

And so Boudicca wordlessly follows me through, and wordlessly picks up a tea towel to help dry the plates and pots and cutlery that Swan's pulling out of the deep, soap-foaming sink.

Swan, Zed and me swap looks over Boudicca's head. This isn't chatting or fun in any way but our newest student is **sort** of joining in with something, which has to be a good sign, right?

"Hey, Boudicca," Zed calls over to our little helper as he dips his hand in the sink. "Catch!"

Zed blows a rainbow-tinted soapy bubble through the circle he's made with his finger and thumb. With a wobble and a tremble, it separates itself from his skin and tumbles around in the soft breeze drifting in through the window.

Boudicca's grey eyes fix on the bubble and the three of us hold our breath. Will she do what she did with the Dory ball and the packet of crisps and let it sail on by? Or will she act like a normal human and hold her hand up to catch it like a delicate blob of a butterfly?

Before we're able to find out, Toshio suddenly barges into the kitchen, a smile a mile wide on his face. The bubble rises in the air and pops.

"Yes! It is OK! Everything is OK!" he announces, holding his thumbs up. "But the goat – it will have to move, I think."

"Is Twinkle on top of Arch's parents' car?" I ask.

"Excuse me?" Toshio asks back, as confused by our conversation as I am.

Then someone else comes barrelling into the kitchen. Someone who can explain it all, by the look of the happy expression on their face.

"Mum and Dad – they say I can stay for a few days!" Arch bursts out. "Lulu suggested it. She said that if it helped give them a bit of space to sort stuff out…"

"So you'll be with me, in MY room," Zed says, his face lighting up at the thought of having a dorm-mate that isn't a goat.

"Yes – the goat must move!" says Toshio, pleased that people seem to understand what he's on about at last.

Arch, understandably, doesn't take too much notice of Zed or Toshio. He's just grinning madly at me, knowing that we will have some precious, best-friend time together.

I walk over to high-five him – but Boudicca gets there first.

She wraps herself tightly round his waist, pressing her head into his chest and beaming an enormous smile of pure joy. Stopped in my tracks, I raise my eyebrows at Arch and shrug. He seems to have found himself a small-girl fan club!

Whatever, it looks like the next few days at St Grizzle's are going to be pretty interesting...

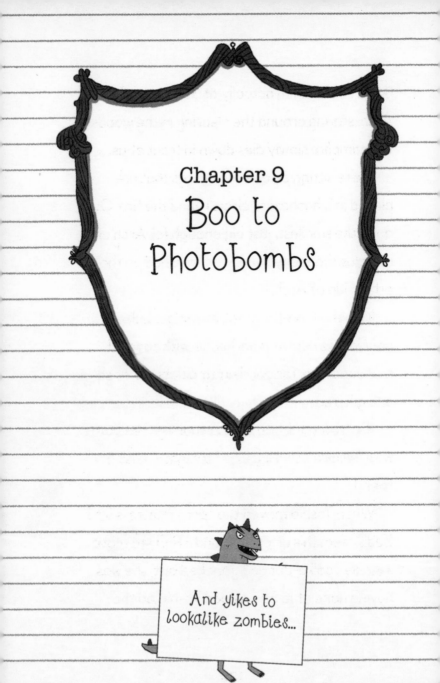

Chapter 9
Boo to Photobombs

And yikes to
lookalike zombies...

"I can't believe I'm actually at St Grizzle's!" says Arch, staring around the clearing in the woods as the campfire slowly dies down in front of us.

We're sitting on one of the logs that are placed in a haphazard circle round the fire. Our one's the smallest, just big enough for Arch and me, plus the teeny super-fan squished on the other side of Arch.

It's been a pretty great evening... Lulu decided we'd have a barbecue with toasted marshmallows for pudding to celebrate Arch being here.

"Do you think you'll mind sharing the room with Twinkle as well as Zed tonight?" I ask my friend.

When Toshio moved the spare mattress into Zed's room this afternoon and TRIED to move Twinkle's polka-dot ~~dog~~ goat bed **out**, she was having none of it. She nipped Toshio on the bottom before snuggling herself down on her bed and refusing to budge. For the last few hours she has steadfastly ignored any shooing or attempted bribery-with-food to shift her, and has "Meh!"ed menacingly at anyone coming near.

"Yeah, sure," Arch says casually.

He doesn't say anything else. Maybe the idea of sharing a room with a sort-of-stranger is making him a bit shy.

"And are you looking forward to lessons tomorrow?" I say, changing the subject. "Lulu says we can start building a new tree house in the morning. Won't that be brilliant?"

"Brilliant." Arch grins, brightening up. "And hey, after classes, we could go off on our own and make some new mini-movies, couldn't we?. And then on Saturday we can have the WHOLE day together. Just the two of us. Sunday, too, till Mum and Dad come to pick me up…"

I smile, though I feel a little niggle of disappointment in my tummy. Making new mini-movies with Arch will be brilliant. And I can't wait to spend time with him, just the two of us. But at the weekend, it IS kind of fun to hang out with everyone here. I was kind of hoping Arch would get a kick out of doing that, too.

"OK, it's nearly bed o'clock – let's head indoors!" Lulu announces, trickling a bucket of water over the glowing embers of the fire.

There are a lot of disappointed "awww!"s but all the pupils start picking up and packing up whatever stuff is lying around the clearing.

"You know, you still look weird without your baseball cap," I tell Arch.

"No, he looks nice," says Boudicca, which is practically the only thing she's said all night.

"Don't know about that!" I laugh. "But here, let's capture a rare hat-free moment…"

As I wrestle my mobile out of my pocket and get ready for a selfie, Granny Viv rounds up the younger classes and steers them towards the school, Boudicca included.

"Ready?" I say, and Arch and I put our heads together and smile.

"Photobomb!" comes a shout, and sure enough – the image on the screen is of me and Arch, with Swan and Zed yelling, arms wide, behind us.

I start to laugh – of course I do.

Then I catch sight of the frown on Arch's face.

"Why did you have to spoil it?" he snaps at Swan and Zed.

"What?" says Swan, frowning herself.

"We didn't mean to—"

"Forget it," says Arch, cutting off Zed's apology. "See you in the morning, Dani..."

Arch stomps off towards the big house while I quickly wiggle my feet into my flip-flops and try to figure out what just happened.

"Sorry, I don't know what's got into him," I apologize to Zed and Swan.

"It's fine, he's had a crazy day," says Swan, waving the moment away with her hand as if it's nothing to worry about.

"But it's not like him to **be** like that," I carry on ten minutes later in the girls' loos, still trying to figure out my best friend's strange behaviour.

"Look, it's cool, Dani," says Swan, holding the door open for me as we head back to our dorm.

"Like you said, his parents are splitting up. His head's going to be a mess…"

It's sweet of her to say but I still feel muddled. And I'm anxious about Zed and Arch sharing a room. Are they over it, and chatting away happily together? Or is Arch still huffing and pretending to be asleep while Zed gets ready for bed and Twinkle snores?

"Is it OK if I turn out the light?" asks Swan, hovering by the switch as I reach my own bunk. "I'm pretty tired."

"Sure," I say. "Night…"

But I'm more wired than tired.

I reach for my mobile on the bedside cabinet and slide it under the covers. In my duvet cave – with no light spilling out to disturb Swan as she snoozes – I watch Arch's odd little loo-roll zombie movie again. I guess I'm looking at it with fresh eyes now I know how he was feeling when he made it. No wonder those little zombies look so blank and gloomy...

I'm just watching it through for the second time when I feel a tiny tug on my pillow.

"Downboy, you shouldn't be in here," I hiss, tossing back the covers.

But the glow of my mobile screen shows up something that isn't four-legged and drooling.

Yikes! I nearly jump out of my skin at the sight of Boudicca standing over me, staring in that strange blank way of hers.

And now I realize what she reminds me of. I hold up the paused film on the screen, and glance from it to Boudicca and back again.

Yep, she's a total ringer for the loo-roll zombie.

"You scared me!" I tell her, once I get over the shock. "What are you doing here? You're meant to be in Otters' dorm!"

"They do secret whisperings. I don't like it. I'm sleeping here," she tells me in her tiny but firm voice.

With that she calmly trots off to a spare bunk and curls up under the covers.

"Er, all right, I suppose," I mumble, hoping I'm not going to have any nightmares about being stalked by starey-eyed zombies, either flesh-and-blood or loo-rollish cardboard ones...

Chapter 10
Good Day, Bad Day,

And losing Boudicca AGAIN. Oops...

"Good morning, good MORNING!" Lulu trills.

Our head teacher's not here in person – her merry voice is blasting through the speaker above the Fungi dorm door. There's a speaker in every room.

As I stretch myself awake I smile, thinking what a shock it'll be to Arch. I didn't warn him about our morning wake-up song!

But then my smile and my stretch fade as I remember my friend's funny mood last night. I hope he's in a better one today...

"Good morning, good morning to YOOOOOOO!"

THUNKKK!

The door under the speaker slams open.

"Girls! Boudicca's disappeared! AGAIN!" Granny Viv calls out.

I prop myself up on my elbows, and blink at the vision of **red**-haired Granny Viv in her bright

green dressing gown and **yellow** Minion slippers. She looks like she's dressed as a traffic light.

"It's not funny, Dani!" she says, misinterpreting my smile. "It's our job to keep Boudicca safe."

"Uh, it's OK – she came in here again last night," I say quickly, feeling a bit hurt by Granny Viv's stern tone.

"Did she?" asks a yawning Swan from her bunk at the far side of the dorm.

"I meant to come and tell you," I explain to Granny Viv, "but I was thinking about Arch and ... and ... I forgot and must've fallen asleep."

Granny Viv's face softens a little.

"Of course. Sorry to snap, Dani, darling. It's just when I saw Boudicca's empty bed in the Otters' dorm just now, I couldn't help worrying."

"Yeah, it didn't really work out for her being in there," I explain. "Maybe she'd be better with the Conkers? They're more grown-up..."

"Maybe. I'll bring it up with Lulu later," says Granny Viv. "So which bunk is she in?"

"The one in the middle, on the bottom," I say, glad that Granny Viv's apologized.

And I get it – when people are worried, they snap. Arch is worried about what's happening with his family so he got a bit snappish last night. He'll be fine today.

"Which one did you say?" asks Granny Viv, walking back and forth, frowning. "Boudicca? Boudicca, sweetheart? Are you awake?"

There are a LOT of bunks in Fungi dorm. Back when the school was old-fashioned and strict, this room would have been PACKED with ten- and eleven-year-old girls. Now it's home to just me, Swan and our uninvited guest.

I groggily get out of bed to help.

"She got into *that* one... Er..." My voice trails away as I see that the bunk is empty.

There is no duvet.

No pillow.

And no Boudicca.

"OK, here's what we're doing," says Granny
Viv, switching into Sergeant-Major Mode.
"Swan, round up the Otters and Newts and help
them search THIS floor. Dani, take the Conkers
downstairs and do a sweep of the ground floor
– Zed and Arch can help. I'll get the adults and
we'll look outside…"

What feels like a nanosecond later, me, Angel, Klara, May-Belle and Yas are thundering downstairs.

For some reason, Blossom ignores Granny Viv's instructions and hurtles past us at top speed.

"You do the classrooms and hall down THAT corridor," I tell the Conkers. "And me, Zed and Arch will do the rooms off THIS one..."

While the other girls turn right, I turn left – and see Blossom disappearing into Lulu's office.

Just then Zed comes wheeling towards me, already dressed. "What's happening? Is something wrong?" he calls out.

I'm about to answer when a voice blasts out of the speakers.

"BOODICKY! WHERE ARE YOU? COME OUT, COME OUT, WHEREVER YOU ARE!" Blossom screeches at ear-splitting volume. **"BOO! WE MISS YOOOOOO!"**

Arch's head pops out from Zed's room, while Twinkle skips by "Meh!"ing loudly, hooves clip-clopping on the tiled floor.

"Could this place get any louder?" he yells above the racket.

"We need to find Boudicca," I say quickly. "She's gone missing again."

"I got that," says Zed, wincing as Blossom continues with her emergency shouting. "Have you tried the Conkers' dorm? Boudicca hasn't been in that one yet, has she? Maybe she's trying it out for size."

"I just asked Angel – they haven't seen her," I tell him. "But the Newts and Otters are double-checking... They're doing the first floor."

"How about the tree house?" Arch suggests as he hoicks up his loose PJ bottoms. "She might have gone there for some peace and quiet..."

He says that kind of longingly and I can't blame him. St Grizzle's is about as peaceful as a motorway next to a construction site at the moment.

"Granny Viv and the other grown-ups are looking in the garden and woods," I say. "We need to check the dining hall and the kitchen and rooms along here..."

"Who's doing the top floor?" asks Arch.

"Well, no one. That's just the teachers' rooms," I reply. "I think they'd have noticed if a pupil had snuck in with her duvet..."

"Yeah, but it's worth a try, isn't it?" suggests Arch. His messy flop of hair is sticking to his forehead in the shape of a question mark.

"Go!" urges Zed. "I can search down here! After I grab the stupid microphone off Blossom..."

Me and Arch take the stairs two at a time. Everywhere is chaos and shouting, but at least Blossom's been stopped.

(**"BOO! PLEASE COME—** Oof!")

When we arrive at last on the top floor, we see that someone has beaten us to it.

A whimpering Downboy is lying flat on his stomach, sniffing madly at a closed door in the corridor.

"Who's room is THAT?" asks Arch, expecting it to belong to one of the teachers. But I know it doesn't. I take a step closer and see that, according to the very antique brass plaque on the door, this room belongs to "Linens".

Now I may not be as smart as brainiac geeks like Yas and Boudicca but I DO know that "Linens" is old-fashioned for sheets and stuff. This must be one of those cupboards that servants used to use. Just like Swan told us on Wednesday, during Boudicca's tour of the school...

"Good boy, well done," I tell Downboy as I gently shove him aside with my leg and pull the door open.

Inside? Well, like Blossom said, it is a bit like a prison cell. But to Boudicca, it's obviously her newly discovered, secret, one-person oasis.

Cos there she is, fast asleep, all nuzzled up in her duvet nest like a little baby squirrel.

"Looks like Goldilocks found the bed she likes best!" Arch grins at me.

And with that grin, I know I've got my funny, sunshiney Arch back. Last night's moodiness? It was just a blip and today is going to be a GOOD day at St Grizzle's for sure...

It has not just been a GOOD day – it has been an EXCELLENT one so far.

After the excitement of losing and finding Boudicca, Lulu decided that we'd have a Fun Friday and do ALL our lessons together, instead of splitting up into form classes.

First up, we did tree-house building, where I took a really funny picture of Arch flexing his muscles with his foot on a log. He almost looked like a proper lumberjack, except for the huge Peppa Pig plaster Granny Viv stuck on his poorly knee yesterday.

Next, it was music, where Lulu

persuaded Boudicca to give us a recital on her violin. We all had to try **really** hard not to laugh, and try **really** hard to resist sticking our fingers in our ears, when it dawned on us that Boudicca hasn't inherited her parents' musical talents...

For lunch Granny Viv made smiley-face sandwiches, which got EVERYONE smiling, except for Boudicca, who just looked confused.

And now we're in our last lesson of the day – art.

Mademoiselle Fabienne has challenged us to make pictures using food. While we all fiddle with dried pasta, peppercorns and glue, she sits strumming her guitar and singing sad French songs with her eyes closed.

"Just a normal afternoon at St Grizzle's?" jokes Arch as he sticks the final piece of macaroni to complete his Eiffel Tower.

"Sure is," I say with a smile and a nod.

Inspired by the ball in Wednesday's useless getting-to-know-each-other session, I have made a cornflake-scaled Dory which I'm about to paint blue. "How's yours going, Boudicca?"

Since Arch gently woke her up in the cupboard, Boudicca's been by his side practically **every** minute, his very own little tag-along zombie. She's sitting as close as can be to him now, so close you could barely slide a piece of food-art-covered paper between them.

Boudicca doesn't seem to hear me.

I go round the table for a peek at what she's doing anyway.

"Wow, that is amazing!" I gasp when I see what Boudicca's made out of egg noodles and raisins. It's a REALLY good likeness of Vincent van Gogh's super-famous *Sunflowers* painting. "Shall I take a photo of it for you?"

"No, thank you," Boudicca mumbles, pulling it closer to her.

My enthusiastic smile melts away and I remember what Boudicca said that first night when she snuck into our dorm – **she doesn't want to have friends**. Not unless they're Arch, it seems...

TWANNNGGGGG!!

Mademoiselle Fabienne strums a final, dramatic chord on her guitar.

"*Alors, mes chers!*" she calls out. "It is that time! End of school! The beginning of *le weekend*! Enjoy!"

With a whoop of hurrahs and a screech of chairs, everyone's instantly on the move.

"So, ready to make a mini-movie?" Arch says to me, looking excited.

"Absolutely! I'll nip upstairs and get the backpack. Meet me in the entrance hall in two minutes," I suggest, then hurry off, thinking that I'll probably be meeting Boudicca in the entrance hall, too, since I doubt she'll let Arch out of her sight.

But back to our filming... Me and Arch have been mulling over ideas all day. We haven't decided on an exact theme yet but we've got the location – the area around the new tree house where there's piles of sawdust that look exactly like weeny-wee sand dunes. Maybe we'll do a Star Wars scene.

I run to the dorm at top speed, grab our bag of actors from under my bed and scurry back down the grand staircase just as fast. Whirling myself round the curve of the banister at the bottom, I nearly career straight into Zed.

"Hey, guess what?" he says, waving me closer like he's got a secret to share. "Mum just told me that since Boudicca seems happy staying in the cupboard she's going to give it a makeover, as a surprise."

"Cool!" I say, thinking how much Boudicca will love it in there. She'll probably hide away inside and refuse to come out. We could take turns delivering classwork and snacks at regular intervals.

"Toshio painted it white earlier and moved in a mattress, and your gran is putting Boudicca's clothes and books and stuff on the shelves," Zed carries on. "Swan's in my room – we're going to make some mobiles of birds to hang up. Do you want to come and help?"

"Sounds like a great idea," I say, thinking that the birds Swan painted on her wall are just about the only thing Boudicca seems keen on at our school. "Sure, I'll help!"

In that moment – even though I had a backpack of ex-toy actors on my shoulder – it's like I've forgotten Arch is at St Grizzle's.

In that moment I've started walking off after Zed.

DINING HALL

In that moment it dawns on me that I'm being watched and I turn to see Arch glowering at me from the doorway of the dining room with an angry, hurt look on his face. His little tag-along zombie is staring EXTRA hard at me, too.

"If you've got BETTER things to do than film with me, then that's fine, Dani. Go right ahead!" Arch rages.

"No... I didn't mean..." I bluster.

"Well, Zed is obviously your best friend now, so, yeah, feel free to hang out with **him**."

"Look, Arch, Zed was telling me about this really cool thing that—"

"It's MY fault," Zed says, interrupting me in his hurry to make things better. "I didn't know you two had plans. I just thought I'd see if Dani wanted—"

"Whatever," Arch says loudly, cutting him off. "Do what you want, Dani. I don't care."

"I want to do our filming, Arch!" I protest, slipping the backpack off and holding it out to him as evidence.

"Nah, don't worry," Arch says in a narky, off-hand way that I've never heard him use before. "I've got someone else to help me make mini-movies. Right, Boudicca?"

Boudicca opens her eyes wide and nods up at him.

And with that Arch snatches the backpack out of my hand and leads the way towards the back door and the garden and woods beyond.

Wow.

Who knew that three, thoughtless little words like "Sure, I'll help" could turn a GOOD day into a BAD day **quite** so fast?

Chapter 11
Watch the Birdie

And mystery horsey tails...

With no set lessons, Saturday mornings at St Grizzle's are pretty relaxed.

Unfortunately I'm NOT RELAXED AT ALL.

I tossed and turned and couldn't sleep last night, and I've woken up late with an ouchy crick in my neck.

"Hi," I say to Granny Viv as I walk into the kitchen and find my grandma gazing out of the window as she washes the dishes, her stripy jumper and jeans covered by an apron.

"Hello, Dani, darling!" she says, pulling her pink rubber-gloved hands out of the water and giving me a big, damp hug.

"Where is everyone?" I ask her.

I walked through the dining room just now and it was empty except for a few dirty breakfast dishes and glasses.

"I think the Conkers are watching a movie on the screen in the art room, the triplets are out on

169

the lawn having a who-can-stand-the-longest-on-one-leg competition by the looks of it and the Newts wanted to have their breakfast 'like owls do'."

"Which means...?" I check.

"Which means they're eating peanut butter on toast up in a tree," says Granny Viv, pointing a sudsy rubber finger at the big oak just outside the kitchen window. "As for the others, Swan popped out to the shops with her mum in the minibus and Zed is playing Xbox in the office with Toshio."

Granny Viv looks long and hard at me before saying something else.

"But I think you're REALLY asking if I've seen Arch ... and sorry, I haven't," she says. "Didn't you two manage to make up last night?"

"No," I say, flopping back against the work surface. "He just blanked me whenever I tried to talk to him."

"He did seem to be giving all his attention to Boudicca ... which was nice for her, I suppose," Granny Viv points out.

"Yeah, very nice," I mumble, although she must know that watching my best friend spend **every** minute of yesterday evening making mini-movies with his tag-along zombie was NOT so nice for me.

First they were out in the woods. After tea (they ate together, away from the rest of us) he was up in Boudicca's cupboard, shooting stuff in there. I kept checking on my phone to see if they'd posted anything on our YouTube channel, but nope.

Later when me and Swan knocked on the brand-new Linens' dorm, Arch had just taken the bird bunting and mobiles we'd made, said thank you on Boudicca's behalf and shut the door on us.

"The thing is, Arch was just being extra-nice to Boudicca to get at me," I say sulkily. "He's jealous of Zed! Can you believe it?"

"Look at it this way, Dani," says Granny Viv, passing me a plate of warm, fresh-out-of-the-oven cookies. "Arch isn't himself right now. He's feeling as if he's losing his parents, and seeing you so settled here with new friends he's probably feeling like he's losing you, too…"

"But he's *not* losing his parents and he's *not* losing me. Things are just … just changing a bit!" I protest.

"And he'll come to see that eventually," Granny Viv says with a nod, like a wise old punk owl. "But your friend is hurting and you might find he's a bit quiet and—"

"SHE'S GONE!" Arch roars at the top of his panicked voice as he tears into the kitchen, clutching an iPad. "I JUST WENT UP TO HER CUPBOARD AND **BOUDICCA'S NOT THERE!**"

"Not AGAIN!" exclaims Granny Viv, rolling her eyes to the ceiling. "Right, before we start organizing another search party, let's think this through for a minute. Arch – you spent a long time with Boudicca last night. Did she say anything? Did she seem as if she didn't like her cupboard after all? Any clues you can think of as to where she might be?"

"Uh, she didn't say much. I tried to get her involved in making the mini-movies but she didn't really join in." As he speaks, Arch throws me a slightly embarrassed look as if to say...

a) I'm sorry I got so grumpy, and

b) it wasn't fun making mini-movies without you.

"And the cupboard, Arch? Did she seem unhappy there?" I repeat Granny Viv's question.

"Oh, no – she LOVES that. Especially the bunting and stuff."

Arch throws me another embarrassed look as if to say...

a) the bunting and stuff was really cool, and

b) I'm sorry I closed the door in your face.

"So you can't think of anything else that could be helpful, Arch?" Granny Viv prompts him.

"No," says Arch, shaking his head. "Well ...

I suppose there COULD be something. Before I went to bed I left my iPad with Boudicca, so she could watch all the films on our channel, Dani. I joked that if she was too shy to make a film WITH me, she could always surprise me by doing one on her OWN..."

"Fire it up, Arch," Granny Viv orders, pointing to the iPad in his hand.

Arch does what he's told and "fires it up". Or at least presses the "on" button.

And there it is.

A one-minute-long film set on a shelf in the Linens' dorm, starring two of Swan's bunting birds.

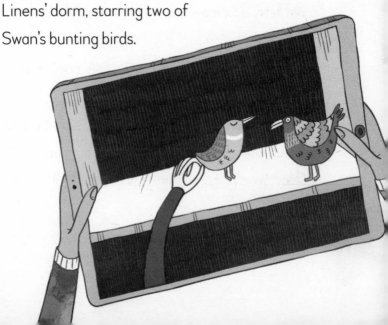

"Are you practising your violin every day, Boudicca?" said one bird, in a deepish, parentish voice. Or at least as deep and parentish as the off-screen Boudicca can manage.

"No," said the smaller bird, in a tiny, high-pitched voice. "I don't like playing the violin. I've told you that but you don't listen."

"Are you practising brushing your lovely hair with a hundred strokes every morning and at bedtime, Boudicca?"

"No. I don't like having long hair. It gets all knotty and in my food. I've told you that but you don't listen."

"Are you settling in at school and making friends, Boudicca?"

"No, because I've never had any before. I don't know HOW to be a friend."

I clutch my chest when I hear what the little bird just said.

Oh, no... That night when I found Boudicca

snuggled in Swan's bunk – I heard it WRONG. I thought she said, in her whispery little voice, that she didn't want to have friends. But now I realize she said something different, and sadder, altogether.

Boudicca has been weird with us all at St Grizzle's simply because she doesn't know HOW to be a friend...

"Well, Boudicca, your schoolwork is more important than friends," the deeper, more parentish bird carries on.

"No, it's not! There is a boy here that I would like to be my friend but I don't know what to say to him. He is SO nice and he looks JUST like Marvin."

"Who on earth is Marvin, Boudicca?"

"The only one who listened to me at home, that's who. I miss him and I want to see him."

"Now don't be ridiculous, Boudicca. You can't go back home."

"Yes, I can! And stop calling me Boudicca. Nobody knows how to say it and I don't like it! I've told you that, too, and you haven't listened…"

The little bird, aided by Boudicca's fingers, flutters and flies off out of shot – and the film stops.

Me, Granny Viv and Arch all stare at each other, stunned at how many ACTUAL words we'd ACTUALLY heard Boudicca speak.

"Do you think she's going to try and make her way back to her house? On her own?" I say, thinking of how teeny-tiny Boudicca will be out in the great big world.

"She wouldn't, would she?" says Granny Viv.

"I think she might have," I reply, with flutters of panic flittering in my chest. "But where IS her home?"

"Hey, won't Toshio have a record of Boudicca's home address in the office?" Arch suggests.

"Good thinking – can you go and ask him, Dani? I'll ring Lulu now to tell her what's happening," says Granny Viv, yanking off her Marigolds. "But how will an eight-year-old girl try and make that journey? Even one as smart as Boudicca?"

I suddenly have a snapshot memory of yesterday, of Boudicca nearly walking into the bus stop cos her nose was buried in Harry Potter.

"I think she might have gone into the village," I announce. "Maybe she'll try to catch a bus? She heard Arch say that's how HE got here…"

"Meet you by Daisy in five minutes," says Granny Viv, talking about her beloved camper van. "And Dani, after you ask Toshio to find the address, can you go and tell Miss Amethyst and Mademoiselle Fabienne that they're in charge?"

"Sure," I call out over my shoulder as I hurry away.

Exactly five minutes later, me, Arch, Granny Viv and Downboy are all piling into Daisy – even if one of us wasn't invited. (Talking about YOU, Downboy.)

"Good luck!" Zed calls out as we slam the doors shut and fasten our seat belts.

"**グッドラック!**" Toshio calls out, too, waving and bowing madly.

We're just rumbling off across the crunching stones of the driveway when Blossom gallops in front of us as if she's doing dressage at a horse show. She's even holding a long swishy tail at her bum.

Hold on...

"Hey!" I yell at Blossom out of the open van window. "What is THAT? The thing you're using for a tail? Where did you get it?"

"It was on the floor of the bathroom! FINDERS KEEPERS!" Blossom yells, before trotting a lap around the statue of St Grizzle and disappearing off round the side of the school.

"Wait, you don't think that was…" Arch begins, going white.

"I hope not…" I mumble.

"Hold tight!" says Granny Viv, and puts her foot down on the accelerator.

VROOMMMM!

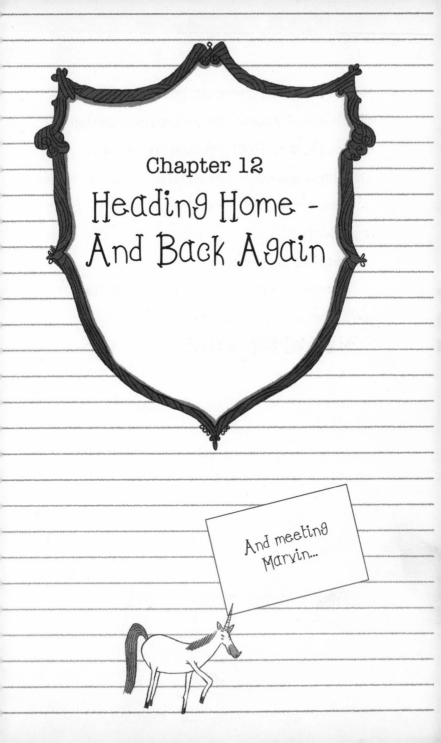

Chapter 12
Heading Home -
And Back Again

And meeting
Marvin...

So we MIGHT be looking for a **bald** Boudicca.

"Any sign of her?" asks Granny Viv, gazing at the bus stop in the distance.

"Nope," says Arch, peering up the road at the shelter. "There's no one there."

And then I spot someone I could do without seeing.

Sneery, meanie Spencer from the local village school. And he appears to be with his surprisingly smiley, sweet-looking mum, who has rosy cheeks, a baby in a buggy and very possibly NO idea how awful her eldest child is...

As we chug up the high street, Spencer frowns at Granny Viv's psychedelic camper van, then frowns his blond eyebrows into a DEEPER v when he spots **me** inside.

OK, he is an idiot but he might be able to help.

"Stop for a second," I tell Granny Viv as I I lean

my head out of the window.

"What, for THAT unpleasant yob?" grumbles Granny Viv, who's no fan of Spencer's.

"Yeah, but that unpleasant yob knows what Boudicca looks like," I explain. "Or at least what she **used** to look like..."

Spencer pulls a worried face as Granny Viv deliberately veers towards him.

"Hi," I call out, above the screech of Daisy's brakes.

Spencer's nostrils flare as if he's just dying to say something rude about one of us Grizzlers. But he shoots a sideways glance at his smiley mum and can't do a thing.

"Er, hi," he reluctantly says back.

"Who's this, Spencie, darling?" his mum asks pleasantly.

"Uh ... someone I know a bit. She's a Griz— She goes to St Grizelda's," Spencer mutters.

"I'm Dani and this is Arch," I say politely, chucking my thumb in my best buddy's direction.

"And I'm Viv!" my gran calls out to Spencer's mother, giving her a wave. "I work up at the school and I've had the pleasure of meeting your boy before."

"Really? How lovely! It's always nice to meet Spencer's friends," his mum says brightly as the baby in the buggy giggles and coos.

Spencer looks like he might be sick, having Grizzlers described as "friends".

"Hey, do you remember the new girl you saw us with on Thursday?" I ask Spencer, since we have no time to waste.

"What – the geek, I mean the *girl* with the book?" he checks.

"Yeah, we're looking for her," I say. "Seen her around the village this morning?"

"Maybe," says Spencer, sounding reluctant with his information. He turns and points back up the road, past the empty bus shelter. "Is that her on the bench there?"

Aha! The bus shelter had obscured the view of the bench just beyond it – and the tiny person sitting on it.

"Yessss! I think it **is** her!" Arch suddenly yelps as he screws up his eyes and stares at the distant small figure.

"You really have SUCH a helpful son," Granny Viv calls out to Spencer's mum, who beams with pride as the van suddenly zooms off up the high street.

In the wing mirror, I see Spencer's disgusted face watch us go. Ha! He must HATE the fact that he's been so helpful to us Grizzlers...

As for runaway Boudicca, she doesn't see us coming, since she has her head in her hands. With her skinny little legs and her luxurious tumble of hair (yay – still there, amazingly), it looks as if someone has left a semi-open furry umbrella leaning against the bus stop bench.

"Boudicca!" I call out of the window, when Granny Viv draws close enough.

"**BOO!**" Arch shouts louder, reaching over me and yanking at the door handle as we come to a stop.

At the sharp sound of her shortened name, Boudicca glances up. Her face isn't blank any more – it's bright pink from crying and her grey eyes are red-rimmed.

Ah, and Boudicca's hair isn't two perfect wavy curtains any more either, I notice – one side has a large clump cut out, leaving a clumsy stump of stubble in its place. It's as if she started cutting her hated long hair then panicked in case she wasn't doing it right.

"Get in, darling!" Granny Viv calls out to her.

After a moment's hesitation Boudicca does as she's told and scuttles in by my side, while Arch jumps over the back of the seat to the one behind so there's room for her.

"Are you cross with me?" Boudicca asks us in her usual mouse-squeak.

"Well, it's not exactly SAFE for you to be taking off on your own, is it, sweetheart?" Granny Viv chides her gently as she nods at me to fasten Boudicca's seat belt for her.

"But Arch did it, when he wanted to see Dani!" Boudicca whispers in her own defence.

"And he shouldn't have. Should you, Arch?" Granny Viv calls over her shoulder to my friend. He doesn't answer straight away – I think he's being licked to death by Downboy, who's deliriously excited to have company in the back with him.

"No!" yelps Arch, trying to fend off the Drool Monster.

"But here's the thing, Boo," says Granny Viv, staring Arch's tag-along zombie in the eye. "We've seen the short film you made. We KNOW you want to go and see your old friend Marvin back home. It's not too far. So, how about we have a little trip there? Would you like that?"

Boudicca's pale-as-huskies grey eyes swim with tears.

"Y-y-yes, please!" she hiccups, then buries her face in my T-shirt.

I'm not sure what I can do except stroke Boudicca's head and pretend she's my dog...

The stroking thing – I've always found it sends Downboy straight to sleep.

And what do you know? I've just found it

ALSO sends troubled and emotional eight-year-olds to sleep, too.

Boo – as we've all agreed to call her from now on – has quietly zzzz'd and drooled down my T-shirt for the whole hour's length of the drive to her house.

On the way, Granny Viv talked to Lulu via speakerphone, to let her know that Boo was okay and what the plan was.

That important call made, Granny Viv, Arch and me passed the time taking wild guesses about WHO exactly Marvin might be. Arch's guess is that he's Boo's old tutor. Granny Viv thinks he's a neighbour's kid. I suspect he might be less alive and that he's actually a beloved teddy or something.

Whoever Marvin is, if coming here helps Boo feel more settled back at St Grizzle's then it'll have been worth the petrol money and the drool stain.

"Looks like this is it!" announces Granny Viv as she pulls up outside a humongous house that you might as well call a mansion. A mansion that looks VERY grand, VERY old, VERY ivy-covered and VERY like it could be the house of a zombie in a horror movie.

"Hey, Boo – we've arrived," I say in my softest, here-we-are-but-I'm-not-sure-about-this-spooky-looking-place voice.

Boo sniffles and snuffles and dreamily blinks herself awake. Then her eyes light up like there are sparkles buried deep in them when she realizes where she is.

"Marvin!" she says, clicking herself free from her seat belt.

"MARVIN!" she calls out, once she's yanked open the camper van door and hopped on to the pavement.

"MARVIN!" she yelps in a nearly normal

person's voice, scanning the skies as she runs into the front garden of the spooky great house.

"BOO!" comes an answering cry.

"See? THERE he is!" yelps Boo, turning to us as she points out her friend. "Doesn't he look EXACTLY like Arch?"

"BOO!" her best buddy calls again to her.

The three of us stare at Marvin.

Well, he's not exactly who ANY of us expected at all...

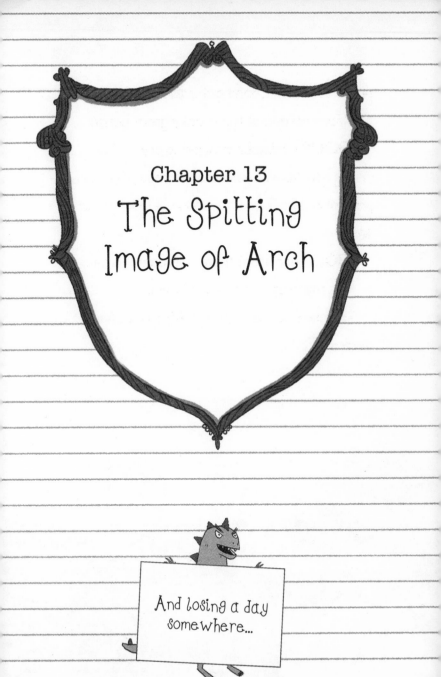

Chapter 13
The Spitting Image of Arch

And losing a day somewhere...

"He's not REALLY like me, is he?" asks Arch.

"You're the spitting image of each other," Granny Viv insists with a grin as she drives us along the familiar country road with the vandalized St Grizelda's sign JUST coming into view.

"Dani?" Arch says in desperation.

"It's the floppy fringe," I tell him.

"It is, isn't it?" Boo says brightly, holding up the pigeon she has clutched comfortably in her hands.

"**BOO!**" coos the pigeon.

"No way!" says Arch, leaning over the back of the seat and studying himself and the bird in the mirror of the windscreen sun visor.

But there really IS a strong resemblance.

It's all to do with some oddly growing feathers in Marvin the pigeon's forelock, if THAT'S what you call a bird's forehead.

In any normal, average pigeon, those three or four feathers should swoop back neatly and tidily against its small head, I reckon. But with Marvin, they stick forward, rockabilly-style.

"If I had my baseball cap on, you wouldn't think we looked alike," Arch insists, sounding slightly freaked at the idea of being compared to a bird.

"Yeah, but what if Marvin was wearing a teeny-weeny baseball cap, too?" I suggest, happy to wind my friend up.

"BOO!" agrees Marvin as we turn into the drive.

Boo beams at her feathered friend and hugs him to her cheek.

On the return journey to St Grizzle's we've learned all about her special chum. Yes, Boo TALKED, using a whole HEAP of words. Amazing, right?

Anyway, it seems Marvin used to regularly land on the windowsill of her lonely classroom-for-one. When her strict tutor and animal-phobic parents weren't looking, Boo would sneak him leftover crumbs from her meals.

She did worry madly about Marvin – he limped, with one stumped foot. Even when he flew, life wasn't easy. Boo would bite her lip, watching as he swooped and swerved with the local gang of crows trying ever more grumpily to drive him from their turf.

Then came the day, not so long ago, when her tutor announced – with great regret – that another family had offered him a vastly HUGE amount more money to home-school THEIR kid.

And pretty immediately after, her parents had looked at boarding school brochures and settled on one that sounded the VERY BEST (ie not too expensive and with no waiting list). Days later Boo found herself with bags packed for St Grizzle's and a knot of worry in her tummy about what would happen to poor home-alone Marvin.

"Anyway, Boo, dear," says Granny Viv as the statue of St Grizzle comes into view. "Remember what I said – Marvin might not want to stay here, no matter **how** nice it is and no matter **how** much you care about him. So please don't be sad if he flies off when we arrive…"

"I know," says Boo, at a regular-person volume, as she idly stares out at St Grizzle with today's makeover of clip-on dangly earrings, blue eyeshadow and Hula Hoop crisps on every stone finger. "But even if Marvin decides to go, that'll be OK. At least he'll understand that I didn't abandon him. Even if we're apart, he'll know that I love him…"

Arch.

Arch and me.

Arch and me lock eyes in the mirror as Boo speaks.

And in that moment it's as if she's speaking about US and not some wee bird-brained pigeon. (No offence, Marvin.)

"Even when you go home tomorrow, you are STILL my best friend," I tell Arch, before I chicken out and the words get stuck behind a lump of shyness in my chest.

"Er ... speaking of when Arch is getting picked up," mutters Granny Viv, spinning the steering wheel round and parking beside a familiar navy Ford Focus, "have we slipped through a portal in time and space and missed a day out somewhere?"

Uh-oh...

After the happiness and grumpiness, after the muddle and making-up, Mr and Mrs Kaminski CANNOT turn up a day early and take my best friend away.

NOOOOOOO!

Chapter 14
Goodbye and Hello!

And the cookies of friendship...

It's time for goodbyes.

So here we all are, the whole school, waving frantically at Arch's car as it crunches over the stones of the driveway and disappears off down the road.

The pigeon perched on the stone head of St Grizzle flaps its wings in fond farewell, too... But as a white streak drizzles down St Grizzle's neck, I realize Marvin was just doing a poo.

"So they're off, then," a voice murmurs beside me. "Wish they'd taken me with them, Dani?"

"Shut up, you big idiot," I mutter, and give Arch a sharp dig in the ribs with my elbow.

Oh, yes, Mr and Mrs Kaminski are heading back home but Arch is very much **NOT**.

His parents came here this morning to have a chat with Lulu. To see if she'd consider having Arch here for the rest of the term while they figure things out.

"If you'd like that, of course, Arch," Mrs Kaminski had said when Arch went to join them and Lulu in her office.

Me, Granny Viv, Boo and Marvin had hovered in the corridor outside, earwigging.

When we heard Arch whoop a loud "YES, PLEASE!", we'd whooped, too, and then everything went a bit bonkers. Boo accidentally let go of Marvin and he flew into the office, flapping around frantically.

Everyone had to duck and take cover while Boo chased him, and Lulu's speech about Arch being very, very welcome at St Grizelda's got kind of drowned out.

"Well, what an exciting morning it's been!" Lulu says now, clapping her hands together and turning to face us all. "Hope there's no more surprises in store. I'm quite worn out!"

"Ahem..." coughs Swan, and we see that she's pointing down at a small, earnest person whose grey-eyed stare is focused on our head teacher.

Uh-oh.

Before they left, Lulu insisted that Mr and Mrs Kaminski have a tour of the school. Granny Viv had gently dragged Boo and Marvin away so that Arch and me could be zombie-and-pigeon-free tour guides.

But what had Boo gone and done in the meantime?

ONLY LET SOMEONE CUT OFF **ALL HER HAIR**!

I glance around for Blossom – random hair-hacking seems right up her street. But the chief Newt is busy feeding some cardboard name-necklaces to Twinkle and looking pretty innocent. What about the triplets then? They're often Up To Something. Last weekend they'd decided they wanted a pet bee and tried to attract one by "borrowing" honey from the kitchen and smearing it on themselves.

And then I spot something. Two somethings, in fact. A flicker of a tell-tale smile on Granny Viv's face and the glint of a pair of scissors sticking out of her trouser pocket.

"My!" gasps Lulu. "What a fantastic new look, Boo! I **love** it!"

Boo breaks into a pleased and relieved smile, and runs a hand through her cropped short hair with its longer flop of fringe.

"Doesn't she suit it?" Granny Viv says brightly as she takes Boo by the hand. "Now, how about you come and try some of the cookies I made **specially** for you this morning…"

At the word "cookies" Blossom drops the name-necklaces and comes scampering. "CAN I HAVE ONE, TOO?" she roars at Granny Viv.

At the same time, without thinking, she reaches out for Boo's free hand.

And, without thinking, Boo smiles.

"Looks like she might be getting the hang of this friend business at last," I say as the rest of the school head inside, too.

Outside, the only ones left are me, Arch, Swan and Zed.

Swan is drawing circles in the stones of the driveway with the toe of her flip-flop. Zed is nibbling at his lip and looking shyly at Arch.

Hmmm… Even with all the sudden sunshine of

happiness around here, there's still a little breeze of awkwardness between my friends.

I'm desperately trying to think of something to say that'll make everything better, when Zed speaks first.

"You look more like yourself now," he tells Arch, pointing at the replacement baseball cap his parents brought along for him.

"Yeah," says Arch. "I **feel** more like myself, too. And that's HUNGRY. Who's up for sneaking round the back and swiping the cookies?"

"Yaaaaayyyy!" yells Zed as Arch grabs hold of his wheelchair and hurtles Zed away at high speed.

Well, when it comes to biscuits and fun, Swan and me aren't going to be left behind.

In precisely no seconds flat, the four of us zoom off in one big friendly blur...

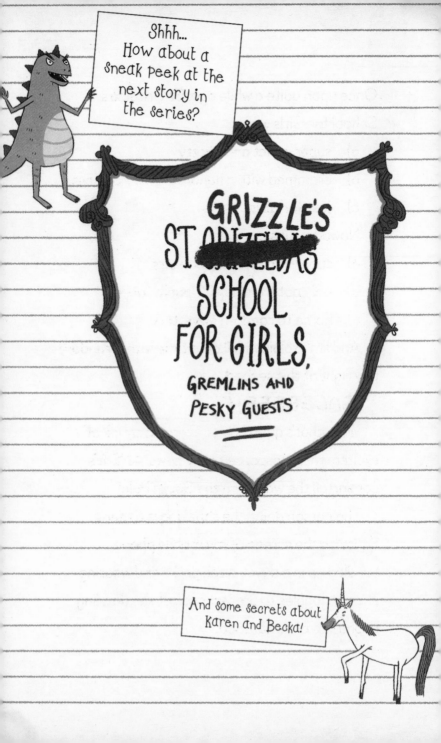

Once upon quite a while ago, St Grizelda's School for Girls was…

a)   super-strict and swotty

b)   crammed with a hundred or more pupils

c)   **just for girls**.

Nowadays it's…

a)   super-fun and a bit bonkers

b)   only got a measly 22 pupils (oops)

c)   home to **random boys**, too.

And I'm explaining all about the **latest** random boy right at this second.

"SQUEEEEE!!"

Wow, that's quite an ear-piercing shriek of excitement in response to my news. AND it's coming all the way from the South Pole!

The person doing the shrieking is a teeny figure on the screen of my mobile phone, bundled up in a duvet-sized parka and wearing chunky goggles to protect against the dazzling brightness of Antarctica.

What with the goofy goggles and the furry-edged hood you can barely see that it's my **very own mum** under there.

"So, quite a surprise, right?" I say, smiling at the screen now that I've spilled the secret I've been saving.

My phone is propped up against the salt and pepper set on a sticky-from-breakfast table in the school dining hall. St Grizzle's – which is what we (nearly) all call it – is tucked in a small pocket of leafy British countryside, a very, VERY long way away from freezy Antarctica. Behind Mum I can see a brilliant blue sky and vast expanse of dazzling white snow. Behind **me** this Sunday morning are cream-painted walls covered with glistening patterns of small, smeary fingerprints.

Oh, and Mum might be able to see a pair of horns too – I can hear the tippetty-tap of Twinkle, the school's pet goat, passing the back of my chair...

But we're talking about surprises here, and at the sound of Mum's shriek, the "surprise" I've just given her **leans** in beside me and waves.

"Hi, Mrs Dexter!" says my best friend Arch.

"Arch Kaminsky, what on EARTH are you doing there?" Mum asks with a confused laugh, clearly all flabbergasted and kerfuffled. "Are you visiting?"

"Nope," says Arch. "I'm going to be at St Grizzle's for the rest of the term – Dani was missing me SO much, she BEGGED me to come!"

Well, that's not **exactly** true, but I'm still super-glad my best buddy is here to keep me company, alongside the OTHER random boy at school – my sweet 'n' shy classmate Zed. We, along with Zed's definitely-NOT-sweet-'n'-shy twin sister Swan, make up Fungi class. We're the oldest in the school, since we're all eleven.

"I can't believe it!" says Mum, slapping a fat, padded glove to her forehead with a dull flump.

"First, your gran and Downboy move in, Dani, and now Arch is there as well?"

You know, I was in a **VERY BAD MOOD** when my zoologist mum dumped me at St Grizzle's a few weeks ago and went off on a three-month penguin-studying expedition. I didn't want to go to a stupid boarding school. I didn't want to be apart from Arch. I also didn't want to be away from my excellently mad Granny Viv or my daft dog Downboy.

But in the end, I didn't have much time to miss Granny Viv and Downboy. One day, some of the younger pupils were convinced they'd spotted a witch with red pom-pom hair living in the nearby woods, but it turned out to be Granny Viv, who – along with Downboy – had come to spy on me and check I was doing alright.

She needn't have worried, cos I **was** alright.

But I'm doing even **better** since Lulu the headteacher offered Granny Viv the job of live-in cook, homework-helper, bedtime story-teller and whatever-else-er-er at St Grizzle's, all because there's a shortage of staff.

There's also a shortage of pupils too, so when Arch turned up out of the blue there was no problem with him becoming a temporary student.

So, yep – me, Granny Viv, Downboy and Arch are all back together again.

In the last few days I HAD thought about messaging Mum and letting her know about Arch joining the gang from home – and about his parents being cool with him staying – but then I thought it would be much more fun to wait till our planned mum-and-daughter video chat today. That way it could be a great big "TA-DAH!" kind of a moment. And everyone loves "TA-DAH!"s, don't they?

"Oh, hello... Who's this?" Mum suddenly asks, leaning in a little closer to her own propped-up phone.

Mum's obviously spotted something I can't see. I quickly turn round, and see that the New Girl has silently appeared behind me and Arch. The New Girl started at St Grizzle's last week too, and like Arch, her arrival was a bit unexpected. However, she DID get dropped off in a posh car by her parents. Arch ... well, he turned up via three buses, a trudge through a marsh, a short-but-frantic chase by a cow and a tight squeeze though a spike-tastically thorny hedge.

"**Boo!**" says the New Girl, in response to Mum's question.

Mum's furry hood tips to one side, as she wonders why a small stranger 16,000 kilometres away might be trying to make her jump.

"Mum, this is Boudicca Featherton-Snipe," I quickly explain with an introduction. "Only she likes to be called B—"

"*SQUEEEEEE!!*"

OK, so that's **NOT** Mum shrieking this time –

it's Boo who's successfully burst my eardrum.

"Ha! NO WAY! Check it out, Dani!" roars Arch, pointing at the phone screen.

With my ear properly ringing now, I notice that the view of Mum has been blocked on HER side by a large, looming, black-and-white head and a pair of circular, staring, yellow eyes.

"**PENGUIN!!**" yelps Boo, who is crazy for anything winged and feathered.

"Oi!" I hear Mum shout, as the big bird starts **clunking** on her phone's screen with its beak. "Leave that alone, you nosey old—"

The phone screen goes blank as the connection is lost.

Uh-oh.

Seems like Mum has been the victim of a fishy-breathed mobile phone mugger...

Karen McCombie

Karen McCombie is the best-selling author of a gazillion* books for children, tweens and teens, including series such as the much-loved 'Ally's World' and gently bonkers 'You, Me and Thing', plus novels *The Girl Who Wasn't There* and *The Whispers of Wilderwood Hall*.

Born in Scotland, Karen now lives in north London with her very Scottish husband Tom, sunshiney daughter Milly and beautiful but bitey cat Dizzy.

Karen loves her job, but is a complete fidget. She regularly packs up her laptop and leaves Office No. 1 (her weeny back bedroom) and has a brisk walk to Office No. 2 (the local garden centre café).

Her hobbies are stroking random cats in the street, smiling at dogs and eating crisps.

You can find her waffling about books, cats and bits & bobs at...

www.karenmccombie.com
Facebook: KarenMcCombieAuthor
Instagram: @karenmccombie
Twitter: @KarenMcCombie

*Okay, more than 80, if you're going to get technical.

Author Factfile

- **Favourite thing about being an author:**
  Ooh, doing school visits, where I can meet lovely real
  people, instead of staring at wordies on a computer
  all day.

- **Second most favourite thing about being an author:**
  Eating cake while I'm writing at Office No. 2 (i.e. my
  local garden centre café).

- **Best question ever asked during an event:**
  "What's your favourite flavour of crisps?"
  (My answer was ALL crisps are good crisps, but ready
  salted will always win my heart...)

- **Tell us a secret!**
  Early on at school, I was rubbish at reading and writing
  because of an undiagnosed hearing problem. From
  the age of five to six, I basically sat in class wondering
  what on earth was going on around me. It took an
  operation and a lot of catching up before I learned to
  read and write well.

- **Favourite waste of time:**
  Dancing whenever I get the chance, much to my
  daughter's shame (like THAT'S going to stop me!).

Becka Moor

Becka Moor is an illustrator/author from Manchester, where they say things like 'innit' and 'that's mint, that' when something is really good. She managed to escape the North for a couple of years and ended up in Wales (which, as it happened, was still up North) where she studied Illustration for Children's Publishing at Glyndwr University. Since moving back home, Becka has set up shop in a little home office where she works on all kinds of children's books, including the 'Violet and the Pearl of the Orient' series and *The Three Ninja Pigs* picture book. When she's not hunched over a drawing or pondering which texture to apply to a dragon poo, she can be found chasing her two cats around the house begging for cuddles, or generally making a mess.

You can find more useless information in these dark corners of the interwebs:

www.beckamoor.com
Twitter: @BeckaMoor
Blog: www.becka-moor.tumblr.com

Illustrator Factfile

- **Favourite thing about being an illustrator:**
  Drawing all day!

- **Second most favourite thing about being an illustrator:**
  Getting to read lots of brilliant stories and imagining
  how the characters might look.

- **Tell us something odd!**
  I have a mug collection so huge that the whole world
  could come to my house for tea at the same time, but
  someone else would have to provide the biscuits!
  I'll have a Hobnob or five, please.

- **Favourite waste of time:**
  Baking. It's only a waste of time because I can't bake and
  whatever comes out of the oven is usually inedible!

Find out how Dani first ends
up at St Grizzle's in...

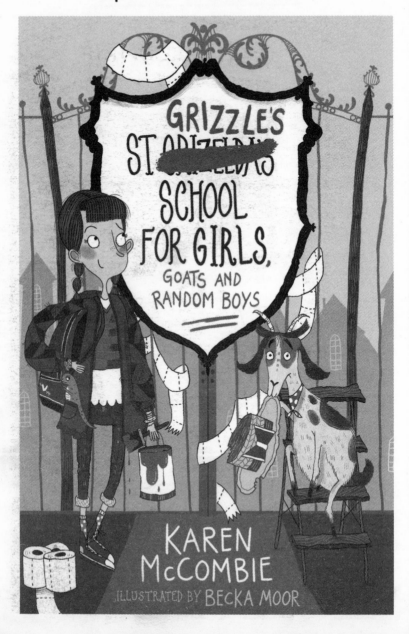

GRIZZLE'S
ST ~~GRIZELDA'S~~
SCHOOL
FOR GIRLS,
GOATS AND
RANDOM BOYS

KAREN
McCOMBIE

ILLUSTRATED BY BECKA MOOR

And what happens next in...

KAREN McCOMBIE

GRIZZLE'S
ST ~~GRIZELDA'S~~
SCHOOL
FOR GIRLS,
GHOSTS AND
RUNAWAY GRANNIES

ILLUSTRATED BY BECKA MOOR

PROPERTY OF
ST GRIZELDA'S
SCHOOL FOR GIRLS